A Love Rekindled

Tad Houlihan

Bloomington, IN   Milton Keynes, UK

AuthorHouse™
1663 Liberty Drive, Suite 200
Bloomington, IN 47403
www.authorhouse.com
Phone: 1-800-839-8640

AuthorHouse™ UK Ltd.
500 Avebury Boulevard
Central Milton Keynes, MK9 2BE
www.authorhouse.co.uk
Phone: 08001974150

This book is a work of fiction. People, places, events, and situations are the product of the author's imagination. Any resemblance to actual persons, living or dead, or historical events, is purely coincidental.

© 2006 Tad Houlihan. All rights reserved.

No part of this book may be reproduced, stored in a retrieval system, or transmitted by any means without the written permission of the author.

First published by AuthorHouse 2/10/2006

ISBN: 1-4259-0950-7 (sc)

Library of Congress Control Number: 2005911304

Printed in the United States of America
Bloomington, Indiana

This book is printed on acid-free paper.

Acknowledgments

For my initial incentive to record this piece of aviation history, once again I want to thank Nancy Provost. Short of her constant prodding I would never have taken the time to sit down with that pencil and yellow pad in front of me and try to tell about some of the great and colorful adventures the airmen of my era experienced.

A number of worldly wise and knowledgeable people assisted in the making of this book. Among them: Nicolai Musante Larsen of Denmark. Nic generously provided me with photographs of the Curtiss C-46 Commando from his marvelous collection of famous airplanes; Malcolm McCrow of Scotland. Malcolm provided photos from his years in Uganda, Africa, and valuable historical information about the area surrounding Lake Victoria and steam ship USOGA. Jerry O'Grady of Ireland. Jerry was most helpful with historical information about County Kerry, and St. Marys Cathedral in Killarney. Laura Eberly of Oregon. Laura's suggestions were very helpful, as always. Roberta Pringle of Montana. Bert's editing, absolutely invaluable, to put it quite mildly. Todd Hunt of Northern California. Todd's graphic artistry is responsible for the book's cover. Finally, I'd like to thank Genevieve, my encouraging, tolerant, and very helpful wife.

Without the unflagging help from each one of these good souls this book could not have been written.

Prologue

JULIA HERJOLFSSON O'Shaughnessy is sitting on the ancient stone bench, her favorite spot, on the high ground overlooking the azalea and rhododendron garden at the peak of their glorious blooming cycle.

Flowers ablaze in the full spectrum of colour with a background in the multiple shades in green so prevalent of County Kerry as in all of dear Ireland. Way off in the distance can be seen the highlands of Macgillycuddy's Reeks beyond Killarney and beautiful Lake Lean.

It is a place and time to reminisce and rejoice, to marvel at life and the gift it truly has been for Julia and the families Herjolfsson and O'Shaughnessy. The tranquility felt from it all and this awesome goodness is heaven to Julia.

It seems like only yesterday that Jamie and Banjo were so unresolved toward building worthy lives for themselves. How blessed were we that the Herjolfsson estate, the dear old family farm back in Minnesota, that had provided so much to four generations of the family, could once again provide the basis from which the lineage could reaffirm their strength and dignity.

That love for home and place had been lost to the boys, for the farm, because of the passing of their mother and father. The warmth and great strength that those two central figures gave through their love and caring was direly missed. Neither son could cope with the dreadful emptiness of life on the old home place without their folks.

The bonding of people and soil, a balanced combination which forms the basis to create those inner feelings required in thinking of a place as home, rather than only a plot of land and a house, no longer held this meaning.

Melancholy and a total indifference toward life appeared irreversible to Julia unless she could think of a way to rekindle the flame of ambition that the boys had initially displayed upon reentering civilian life after World War II duty as pilots with the Royal Canadian Air Force.

Now, here in this most heavenly and serene place, replenshing a contentment she never could have dreamed possible in her past life her thoughts drifted back to that agonizing time of the decision to sell or not to sell the old family farm, the rock solid symbol of strength and hope. The bountiful giving the place had offered to so many throughout all those years, and years, and generations of the proud Herjolfssons, of America, could best serve the family now through it's market cash value in reinvestment dollars that would be compatible to the time and needs of the situation.

Julia's anguish back then, though quite legitimate for the time, seems utterly ridiculous in retrospect to how correct her decision had become....in time.

Though this story is a work of fiction the characters and events are based upon actual happenings as related to this writer by the brothers, Herjolfsson, themselves. The time setting was within post war years 1945 through the 1960's.

Jamie, Banjo and their aunt symbolize some of the people of that era following World War II and into the age of Jet Airliners.

One

THE BROTHERS: Leif James 'Jammie' Herjolfsson and Bjarni Joseph 'Banjo' Herjolfsson, in the year 1955, seem content to eke out a bare subsistence at the 'Viking Retreat'.

At this sleazy tavern in rural Minnesota, Jammie is the backroom card shark of an illicit poker operation.

Banjo, the younger of the two brothers, works as the tavern's entertainment with his banjo, and does the janitorial work.

Both are good natured, big hearted, above average in intelligence, but shiftless.

Aunt Julia, heiress to the old Herjolfsson family farm, is a retired high school teacher from nearby Red Wing, Minnesota. Aunt Julia, never married, had dedicated her life to her work. She was now living at the old home place on the family farm, with nothing better to occupy her mind than her dear brother's two sons. Though Julia dearly loved her nephews, she was more than a little angry at them over their lack of gumption, and she was also embarrassed by the blight to family Herjolfsson's name that they had created. Ever since 1950, when Julia's brother Eric had died suddenly, the farm had gone to seed, as did Eric's two sons, it appeared.

Without their dad, the boys had no stomach for the backbreaking , heartbreaking, farm life.

To drown their sorrows over the passing of their beloved father, the last of their parents, they drifted into spending more and more time at the 'Viking Retreat'.

Finally they moved into the tavern, sharing a small room in the storm cellar.

During the World War II years, both brothers, anxious to join the fight and high adventure, with an equal excuse to escape from farming and the isolation of rural life, had gone to Canada to join the Royal Canadian Air Force.

Jammie, the more independent and rebellious of the two, spent the war piloting twin engine night fighters.

Banjo ended up as a squadron commander of four engined Lancaster bombers.

Both brothers had distinguished themselves as combat pilots.

At war's end, returned to civilian life, they had tried unsuccessfully to land a civilian flying job that lasted more than a few months before the small, under financed, nonsched airlines would fold. Usually these struggling airlines were formed by unemployed ex military pilots who would team up, cash in their war bond savings, buy a war surplus DC-3, and run out of operating capital within three to six months due to poor management, lack of business experience, and more often than not, their first engine failure or some other expensive mechanical problem.

The brothers had tried nonsched piloting for a few years, with nothing to show for their effort. Most outfits had gone belly up owing them anywhere from a month to three months in back pay. Each new flying job was like shooting craps, you had to roll the dice to take a chance on coming out winners.

Some new outfits, with the right backing and everything else in their favor, did come out winners. Jammie and Banjo weren't lucky enough to have made it into a seat with one of the winners. Broke, disillusioned about aviation, they had returned to the farm and worked there with their father until his death, shortly there after.

Looking at the sadly neglected fields, the acres and acres of land needing to be plowed and harrowed then sowed with new seed prior to any chance for pain filled harvest and reward Julia suddenly envisioned Jammie and Banjo. How sadly similar were the neglected and raunchy looking fields to how she had suddenly envisioned her nephews.

Finally, on one fine spring morning while sitting on the porch in her favorite rocking chair Julia had an inspiration. The boys needed a push. Julia decided there and then, at that very moment, to sell all the farm land, keeping only the plot that the home stood on, and with the cash she would form a three way partnership with the boys.

She would let them decide on the kind of business they would like to go into, the profits of which they would share three ways. Losses would be a two way deal, Jammie and Banjo would have to cover any losses.

If there were eventual profits Julia's share would go into her personal savings account at the bank. This money would serve as reserve for any unforseen problem that might arise, an emergency source of ready cash to be available in dire circumstances.

However, the boys wouldn't know about this safe guard. Not until all else had failed, and only then, would she reach out. Julia's thinking on this subject, though a bit painful, was well intentioned toward forcing her nephews to use good judgement at all times.

Two

JULIA EASILY sold the farm land, at a very good price, then asked the nephews to come for an important talk.

As it turned out, much to Julia's pleasure and relief, the boys quickly suggested a plan with merit. They advised Julia of a set of recent developments in India and the United States that, if linked, could offer them entry into the cargo aircraft leasing business.

The brothers believed that direct entry into airline operation was too risky, but the leasing of aircraft to companies currently established and in possession of route franchises was a sound business. Many airlines had seasonal requirements for additional planes, and in the development of new routes, leasing was the most economical and convenient way to operate.

Jammie and Banjo believed that the recent availability of Curtiss C-46 cargo planes being offered for sale by the government of India, at prices approximating that of their weight value in aluminum scrap metal, combined with the very recent need by American medical research laboratories for hundreds of Rhesus monkeys to be flown from India to the U.S.A., could offer a once in a lifetime opportunity to pull off a business coup.

The C-46s, part of an enormous fleet of WW II planes that had been utilized on the Army Air Force's China-Burma-India air supply route over Burma's jungles and the high and treacherous Himalaya Mountains, (the operation commonly referred to as the **"CBI Hump Airlift"**), had been given to India at war's end. India had by now developed their airline services to the point they no longer needed old WW II equipment and were upgrading into modern airliners.

The coincidental timing of this factor and the break through on finding a vaccine for Poliomyelitis, with the Rhesus monkey of India playing a major part in research and development of the vaccine, was the key to the plan.

In theory, the brothers figured, they could buy a C-46 for next to nothing, (nothing, that is, when the same plane is compared to what it would cost in the States), load it up with monkeys, fly to the U.S.A., and end up with a viable tool to build a business.

If all went perfectly the trio could end up with a C-46, in the U.S.A., at an investment totally recovered upon delivery and payment for the monkeys.

Estimating the costs, as close as was possible from all available information, it appeared a sound business idea to Julia, and she gave her blessings to her nephews.

The partnership was duly established and the great adventure for the Herjolfssons' was on.

More than any other reason, Julia gave her consent to the scheme because she noticed a sparkle, a revitalization, to the spirit of Jammie and Banjo she couldn't remember ever seeing before. Even though the project sounded risky, a real long shot, there was now an enormous aura of power emanating from the brothers that tended to overshadow any doubts the boys weren't going to manage to pull this off. They were emotionally super charged to a point where performing miracles even seemed quite possible now, and as this uplifting power surge overflowed to Julia, a more positive feeling emerged toward her nephews for the first time in years. She also caught the feeling of excitement for this great adventure that lay ahead.

Jammie and Banjo, after sitting in the airliner for only a short time while enroute to India, began to feel the pangs of realism setting in. They both knew that what they were attempting to do was one hell of a giant gamble.

To fail was to let down the only person in the world who believed in them and loved them dearly. To let that wonderful old lady down would be horrible beyond belief. Just sitting there thinking about all the ramifications of what failure would mean was terribly nauseating

They were going to have to prove what it is to be of Viking stock....Julia certainly came forward with what she is made of. Now it was up to them to carry this thing through **successfull**y, no matter what.

Arriving in India trouble became the fourth partner. Totally out of their depth in old world ways of doing business they soon discovered how difficult it is to perform the task of buying something, anything.

At every turn there were middle men, all of whom had a price. Paperwork transactions were a nightmare of frustrating methods used to shakedown fees for the, seemingly, endless stamps of approval required in order to secure access to the next "official" step. A process (theoretically) leading to successful conclusion of what one originally had set out to accomplish, but in the time and money consuming hassle one has the tendency to just go along with the "rip-off" just to get it over with as soon as possible and end the torture. Those old-world bureaucrats were amazingly adept at legally robbing one blind, and they usually did so with the kind of smile that lets you know how great their delight was in putting you through their little games of power play.

Before they realized it they had gone through considerable amounts of cash, mostly in the form of bribes, all through the extremely lengthy process of purchasing the airplane. Time was being consumed at an alarming rate and they still had nothing concrete to show for it.

When patience finally wore out there was a scene, best described as a yelling match, between Banjo and a clerk at the Ministry of Transport, ultimately leading to Banjo's arrest and confinement in the local hoosegow.

Jammie, in turn, spent the better part of a day in effort and considerable cash getting Banjo bailed out of jail, and considerable more cash in restitution payment to the clerk's "damaged pride". The incident cost them an additional day and a half slippage in their originally planned calendar, now a full three weeks behind schedule, and they still didn't own a Curtiss C-46 'Commando'.

The brothers did, however, have a briefcase filled to capacity with paperwork, certificates, and all kinds of beautifully ornate and colorful looking stamps and official government seals.

At one point in the over all ordeal it seemed they were going to have more money wrapped up in paperwork than the value of the airplane itself.

Finally, about six weeks into their learning process on how stressful life can become when one decides to purchase an airplane in a country as screwed up as India, they had possession of their C-46.

She was by no means anything approaching airworthiness condition due to her many years of exposure to the ravages of India's heat and idleness. Serious concern started to settle in when they became aware of the numerous hydraulic fluid and engine oil leaks, seemingly, coming from everywhere. Hose assemblies, engine accessories, and fittings throughout each engine were leaking due to loose clamps, bolts, and gaskets and seals that had dried out and deteriorated.

Another ten days of changing numerous hose assemblies, replacing gaskets and seals, tightening bolts, lubricating countless bearings, servicing every grease fitting, and eventually reaching a point where the brothers felt there was nothing further they could do to prevent them from sucking in their guts, climbing aboard their old bird, and getting the show on the road.

Their flight to collection point for the monkeys went reasonably uneventfully with the exception of some more oil leaks which they attempted to handle in basically a 'jury-rig' fassion.

Three

As IN the airplane purchase hassle, the brothers ordeal in the monkey buying process was just another miserable exercise in being compelled to cope with a mass of pathetic con artists and downright beggars. Simply put, Jammie and Banjo's "grand adventure" was steadily losing a lot of it's original charm and appeal.

Through the exasperating experience buying the monkeys, fuel and oil, paying for airfield parking fees, commercial handling service fees for the actual loading of several hundred monkeys in cages holding five or six animals each, the brothers had nearly forgotten about food and water the animals would need.

In an effort to accomplish this final task quickly the handling company was requested to rush an order of assorted fruits and containers of water aboard along with enough tin cans to provide each monkey cage with it's own water container.

Within only a couple of hours, but a period of time that seemed endless to Jammie and Banjo as they contemplated the takeoff and actual commencement of their tremendously momentous undertaking, the truck arrived with the food and water supplies. Bananas and other assorted fruits and greens were contained in large crates, nearly a thousand pounds of extra weight, and duly loaded aboard. Much of this load ended up in the forward part of the plane, the small room just aft of the flight deck or cockpit, commonly referred to as the radio operator and navigator's compartment.

At last ready to depart India, the brothers cranked up the engines, taxied the plane to the runway, and were about to apply power for takeoff when they glanced at each other. Both men were sweating profusely in the small confines of the flight deck, not merely from the terribly hot climate of that summer day in India, but also from their dreaded thoughts of what their odds were that they'd actually pull this risk filled gamble off. Here they were, seconds from lift off for the greatest adventure and gamble of their entire lives, to date.

"Jammie, I hope you're doin' like me...prayin this old girl can be coaxed into haulin' us and those screamin' animals all the way to U.S. of A." Banjo said, from the pilot seat, as Captain for this first leg of their trip homeward bound.

"Banjo, I'm not only praying for that, I'm askin' the big man upstairs to please overlook the fact we're terribly overloaded, and to keep in mind that we're exhausted, broke, and besides, Auntie Julia is countin' on us to hack it."

At that they both laughed nervously, then with very solemn expressions, shook sweaty hands and prepared to apply maximum takeoff power to the old, but always reliable, Pratt and Whitney R2800, 2,000 horse power engines.

Banjo, his hands soaking wet, advanced the throttles forward ever so gingerly, all the while listening intently for any strange sound or off beat vibration that would indicate trouble somewhere within the thousands of moving metal surfaces, bearings, gears, and assorted mechanical parts, all laboring furiously to accomplish flight.

At first the exceedingly strong beat of his heart could be heard and felt in his ears, but as more and more power emerged from those wonderful old engines, their sound and corresponding power thump soon overrode the sound of his heart beat. It happens at times like these when a kaleidoscopic like surge appears within ones psyche, a blend of deeply soulful inner peace all mixed in with supreme excitement, joy, and anticipation for the sheer exhilaration that flight represents to those of us human beings who have chosen to soar with the eagles.

The engines sounded like beautiful music to both men, continuing so throughout takeoff, climb to cruising altitude, and level off. After reducing power to a minimum for long range cruise Banjo leaned toward Jammie, and said: "Bro, she sounds like a symphony orchestra playin' beautiful music, doesn't she!?....and, you know, she feels more like a young and spirited girl than the weary old lady she really is."

Jammie, who was now busily engaged in trying to get organized in his copilot duties involving navigation and radio communications, had his lap covered with paraphernalia of the job; clipboard with the flight plan and routing log sheets, navigation charts, International Flight Information Manual, his Jeppesen circular computer, and the worried frown on his brow from all those unknowns that were certain to be lurking somewhere up ahead.

" Banjo, my dear little brother, your C-46 is simply an elderly machine we've called out of retirement from it's place of a deserved and well earned rest. Like a lot of women you never can be sure of their real intentions,....what they've got up their sleeve, so to speak!" After a rather extended period of thought, Jammie continued: "What we've got here is not, as you so eloquently put it; 'a young, spirited, and pretty little girl'....we've got us a **great big bull by the horns**, and I think it'd be best we think of it in those terms....at least till we get back to the States, dear little brother."

"I guess I got a little carried away, Bro...Counta' bein' we're up here in our own big old bird, chuggin' along toward our whole future....every minute and mile closer to pullin' this fantastic thing off....you know what I mean!" Banjo said this in a tone of voice filled with emotion and close to tears over the weight of the words he, himself, had just spoken.

The flight plan called for a non-stop flight to Abadan, Iran in the theory and hope for cheap fuel and oil. A war one time buddy of Jammie's was based there heading up Iranian Airways's aircraft maintenance facility. The airline's Persian Gulf division had been established there principally to support Iran's 'National Iranian Oil Company' with their transportation requirements to and from the numerous field production sites and cities within the Gulf region. The city of Abadan, it's giant oil refinery, modern seaport, and International Airport were all built in support of this major supplier of petroleum products to the world.

Bat Marlow would help out in event there were any maintenance problems to deal with and he might even loan them enough money to cover their fuel and oil expenses, Jammie assured himself. Bat had served as Jammie's crew chief when they were assigned to a Beaufighter squadron in the North African campaign. Fighter pilots and their crew chief's often become very close, and not all that different than blood brothers. It's a relationship each man earns from mutual respect and understanding of the others part in the serious game of war time combat operations. The life or death of a pilot can actually depend upon the skill, integrity, and soul of the man responsible for the airworthiness of his airplane. Consequently, lifetime bonds are often forged under relationships of this sort. Jammie and Bat truly qualified in this facet of the brotherhood of flight.

Though more than a year had passed since they last communicated via the mail, Bat was definitely of the old school: The era of "**The brotherhood of airmen**", that uniquely strong friendship all people felt toward one another in the aviation game, where a helping hand was always there when a brother airman was in need. Whether it exists in this day and age is doubtful, but during that first half century of mans love affair with flight we were definitely all birds of a feather, and we stuck together as a matter of survival.

After Abadan the next stop would be Amsterdam where both brothers had WW II friends flying for KLM, the Royal Dutch airline, and again they would be obliged to ask for assistance from friends. The unplanned heavy drain on their finances while agonizing their way through the bribery and extortion practices of doing business in India had reduced their billfolds to practically nothing, and they weren't even to Abadan yet.

It was about two hours after leveling off at 4,500 feet, their initial cruising altitude, where they would be compelled to remain until enough fuel weight had burned off, thereby allowing for a resumption in climb to reach their planned cruising altitude of 8,500 feet, a much more economical and cooler long range cruising altitude. At 4,500 feet

the cylinder head temperature gages were both indicating about 232 degrees centigrade, the very top of the green operating arc, way too hot to feel comfortable sitting there waiting to become light enough to start creeping up in a 'cruise climb' power setting to those cooler outside air temperatures above.

Jammi and Banjo were really sweating it out now, eyes glued to the high engine operating temperatures and correspondingly low engine oil pressures, where both oil pressure gages were flaunting their fluctuating needles at around 70 pounds per square inch, 5 psi into the red radial line on the gages. It's times like these that ones ass starts to really bite into ones seat cushion, when the most minute period of time seems endless.

Finally, it was agreed their gross weight was close enough in fuel-burn-down to start the cruise/climb to 8,500. The rate of climb was to be performed at a very shallow 150 feet per minute and at engine power settings applicable to their density altitudes as they ascended.

Arriving at 8,500 about twenty eight minutes later and with the free air temperature gage reading 77 degrees F, thirteen degrees cooler than the 90 degrees the engines had been laboring under at 4,500 feet, the cylinder head temperatures started to cool down after several minutes in stabilized level flight, gradually backing down a bit from the menacing 232 degrees that were torturing the poor old engines.

Though the 'free air temperature' gage reflected the outside air temperature accurately

it did not represent the additional heat generated inside the plane from numerous radios, electrical inverters, and hundreds of monkeys. The cockpit temp had been hovering around 100 degrees at 4,500 feet. Now, at 8,500 it was down to a more liveable 84 degrees.

As night arrived, just as they were leveling off at 8,500, the temperature dropped a few more degrees, hence a bit easier burden on man, machine, and monkey to endure the long journey to Abadan.

The thin air of 8,500 feet, combined with temperatures in the eighties, and starting out on the trip in a less than rested condition, this long night was going to be a bear cat. Every airplane type has it's own distinctive power thump, sound, and feel. The C-46 was blessed with wonderfully relaxing characteristics. Cockpit complacency could easily set in on the crew from this mesmerizing effect, and as darkness fell, the airplane now flying on automatic pilot, it wasn't long before both brothers succumbed to the inevitable.

===== A Lineage Rekindled =====

Fatigue, night, anoxia, and the soothing old C-46 had combined to put the crew to sleep. The plane droned on into the night for nearly an hour before it entered an air mass of much cooler air. Where these two unlike air masses met, turbulent air started buffeting the plane around enough to bring the crew back to startled consciousness. Now, wide eyed and fully awake, the brothers looked at one another and though neither uttered a word, it was obvious this would never happen again. Facial expressions had said it all, words would simply have been overkill.

While Banjo hand flew the plane through the moderately choppy air, getting her back on track after having drifted considerably off course during their 'siesta', Jammie decided it was time to get out of his seat and move around a bit while checking the tie-downs on the monkey cages. Then the thought of cages full of monkeys flying around back there in the cabin of the now bucking and tossing plane, combined with a real possibility there could be monkeys running amok, furthered to stimulate Jammie's adrenalin, now increasing his senses fully.

No sooner had he left the flight deck and entered the adjoining radio and navigators compartment when Banjo heard a loud and clear: **"Holy Sheeeeitt"**!!!! from Jammie.

Startled and turning quickly in his seat to look back toward Jammie he saw his brother coming toward him, walking backward very slowly.

"What the hell's happened, Jammie…monkeys get loose?"

"We've got a god damned **snake** aboard…it's right on top of one of those crates of bananas…spitting at me…Now isn't that just one dandy little situation!!!???" Jammie said

in a tone of voice several octaves higher than usual.

"Get the fire extinguisher, the CO2…give him a shot of that stuff!!!…it oughta' freeze him in his tracks, don't you think?" Banjo shouted back at his brother, at the same time feeling the hair on the back of his neck standing straight out, and as hot as it was in the cockpit, he felt a chill run up and down his spine.

Jammie immediately turned around and jerked the fire bottle from it's hold-down fixture at the cockpit entrance way. Cautiously he proceeded toward the menacing reptile, fire extinguisher extended at arms reach and in readiness. Now, with the bottles nozzle extended to it's full reach, some 18 inches, Jammie proceeded forward to do battle out of Banjo's line of sight. Banjo couldn't put the plane back on autopilot as it was too turbulent for that, it had to be hand flown. He couldn't help his brother other than try to maintain the bucking bronco of an airplane in as level and stable a flight condition as humanly possible, wondering all the while what they'd do if the damned snake made it's way into the cockpit.

Jammie approached the snake at a snail's pace, extinguisher nozzle aimed directly at the Cobra's upraised, fully hooded, and hissing head. At about two feet separation between nozzle and the yellowish brown colored snake it struck out at the nozzle. Jammie pulled the trigger at that same instant and held it open for a full five or six seconds. This created a large cloud of frozen moisture which obscured the snake from view. There was a moment of sheer terror after the cloud cleared when Jammie noticed the snake was no longer atop the crate of bananas. He instinctively jumped backward, in escape, crashing against a bulkhead stantion and dropped the fire bottle as a result.

"What the hell's happening?...the son-of-a-bitch get you, Jammie?...are you alright?"

"Oh, there the son-of-a-bitch is...frozen solid....on the floor!" Jammie spoke in a manner more as if talking to himself.

"You're okay, Jammie?" Banjo asked again, with a high degree of concern to his tone.

"Yea...I'm okay...where's the fire/crash axe...I'm going to chop that fuckers head off...Banjo...where's the axe?" Jammie asked, his voice sounding a bit more normal now.

"It's right there, above your head....near where the fire bottle was hanging!...see it?" Banjo said.

"Bang!...Bang!...Bang!...Bang!...Take that you nasty little turd!" Jammie said in a very loud voice.

"Jammie, for Christ sake, come here!...what the hell you doing, choppin' the airplane to pieces?"

"My dear little brother, I needed to make sure he wasn't just dazed or something, so I did what had to be done." Jammie spoke in a matter-of-fact manner.

"Sounded like you were killing a whole bunch of em back there."

"Maybe there are a whole bunch of em on board this old crate...don't they travel in pairs?...I mean, I've heard they do... Nice load of fruit we've got, isn't it, Bro!?" Jammie said.

"Could the bugger have been aboard before?...I mean, it could have been living in the plane back there at the storage field...Remember all the bird nests they found while unpickling her, and during the inspection work?" Banjo said as he labored at the controls to maintain some semblance of level flight. Air turbulence was gradually worsening and now they could see lightening flashes up ahead a hundred miles or so.

"I'm goin to try once more to get back to the cabin. Your cousins may be in for a cage busting ride real soon now, judging by the fire works we're charging into, and I'm taking my trusty fire bottle and axe with me for protection....just in case...See you later...I hope." Jammie said with a grin.

"Be careful, that's a God damned jungle back there, and you're no great white hunter!..One little old Cobra and you go ape shit and start tearing the plane to shreds." Banjo said, then laughed uproariously at his own idea of a joke.

This provoked Jammie into sliding the dead snake's head onto the blade of the fire axe and bring it up to hold in front of Banjo's face.

"Get that damned ugly thing outa' here you crazy bugger... I hate snakes...dead or alive, Jammie. I'm going to get even with you for that...Jesus what a dumb trick," Banjo yelled as he squirmed back in his seat as far away from the mean looking killer as possible.

Jammie, smiling, then departed for the depths of their private little jungle aloft.

Most tie-downs needed tightening and some cages needed repositioning to better ride out the rough looking storm up ahead. By the time he finished securing things and had made his way to the cockpit, the airplane was being tossed around the sky like a toy. The storm had engulfed the brothers, their C-46, and their hundreds of terrified little passengers. The whole trip was a bonafide nightmare.

Finally, after nearly twelve hours of bouncing around the sky, some of it in severe turbulence, smoke and haze from Abadan's giant oil refinery appeared on the early morning's horizon.

After landing and parking near National Iranian Oil Company's aircraft maintenance hangar, Jammie looked over at Banjo's haggard face and couldn't help feeling a great surge of pride and affection for his younger brother, and for what they both had accomplished. Leg number one of their flight homeward bound, in their own C-46, was completed successfully.

As the engines shut down, their melodious sound now silenced, a different sound disrupted the brothers euphoria. A chorus with hundreds of highly excited little voices filled the atmosphere now with a startling urgency. Down to earth again in jolting sobriety, the brothers looked at each other for a moment while taking in the clamorous sound of their charges two bulkheads aft.

A big smile emerges on Banjo's face as he says: "So far so good...eh big bro?" Then he unbuckled his seat belt to face the next phase of their responsibilities.

The monkeys were hungry, thirsty, tired, frightened, and apprehensive about this latest sudden change to their lives in captivity. They too had been tranquilized by the soothing murmur of those magnificent old Pratt and Whitney R-2800 radial engines.

After the feeding and watering chores were completed, the animals now reasonably content, the brothers deplaned and met the N.I.O.C. maintenance crew just now arriving for work, with sun already beginning to prove it's summer time frenzied power here in a part of the earth where daytime summer temperatures can reach 150 degrees, and an average day time temperature is often around 143 degrees, (in the shade, that is).

Though still quite early in the day the tarmac was soft and nearing that point it would stick to ones shoes.

Bat Marlow seemed overjoyed to meet his war time buddy, but after a few moments of updating their years since WW II, Bat suddenly cut Jammie off from their combined reverie of the good old **'dark'** days way back then, and those of the much less glamorous and memorable of recent times: "Jammie, you've gone to hell....literally, you're in **hell's kitchen**, here in your aluminium bucket...here in dear Abadan! This is, believe it my friend, living hell, and your bloody animals are not long for this world if we stand here beating our chops any longer," Bat said with finality.

"Bat, we've got some oil leaks we'd sure appreciate you looking at...need to know if you think we could go on to Holland with em'...fix em' there!?... If so, we'll fuel up and shag ass outa' your little Garden of Eden here... But I've gotta' be honest... they look real unhealthy to my brother and me... to be taken' a chance on, I mean." Jammie said this haltingly, with a slight grimace, and in a low tone of voice that quite effectively relayed his sincere anxiety.

"Let's take a look, **Flight Leader...sir!**" Bat said in jest. "Probably every seal in the old derelict is shot...What's it been ten, maybe twelve years drying out in putrid old India?" Bat said, as they proceeded toward the left engine.

As they stood there staring at multiple oil streaks trailing out from the cowl flap doors, ugly black oil all the way back over and under the wings, and even dripping off the horizontal stabilizer, Bat couldn't help starting to laugh uproariously.

"I am sorry Jammie, it truly is not a funny sight...In fact it would be more apropos to label this scene a bloody disaster area!" At this they all started laughing like a bunch of wild hyenas.

After this shock induced outburst had subsided somewhat, Jammie, in a serious tone came out with: "Yea, but at least the engines ran great...along with everything else... systems wise, that is....Heck, she operates a hell of a lot better than she looks, Bat...at least there's that going for the old girl!"

"Oil leaks?...Bloody fucking hell, you've got multiple gushers here, Jammie boy. You are not going to Holland today, and it's too hot to work on the aeroplane during the bloody heat of day. We do our outside work at night after the bloody metal cools down enough to allow us to work without gloves... What we have here, Jammie, is a problem of rigging up a way to cool the cabin of your zoo enough to prevent the animals from cooking their bloody fucking brains out!" Bat said, his eyes wide open, and with an expression a person displays when deep in thought over how to solve a life threatening problem complicated by the need for immediate action.

Jammie could almost hear the gears turning and churning away inside Bat's agile brain as he observed this ingenious engineer standing there, hands on hips, staring into space as he searched for the answer buried deeply within his memory bank.

A Lineage Rekindled

Time flashed back in Jammie's mind to a scene that took place many years ago on a Libyan desert. There, in his minds eye, was Bat standing in front of the Beaufighter that Jammie had barely made it back to base in after his plane had been shot up by the rear gunner of a German JU-88.

Everything about the scene was terribly reminiscent, sort of deja-vu, everything with the exception that instead of the handsomely rugged features of a very young ex college soccer player standing there in his RAF issue khaki desert shorts, shirtless, but wearing hobnailed army boots, and pith helmet, this Bat was much older looking now, quite thin, and he now wore standard Middle Eastern summertime apparel; the impeccable white shorts, white shirt with sleeves rolled up to the elbow (but definitely not above elbow height), knee high white stockings, and locally handmade buffalohide sandals.

This man was the same good man he'd always been, just older, wiser, and wearing clean whites instead of the dirty grease stained khaki standard of North Africa's RAF airplane mechanics back then when those dedicated fellows often worked around the clock to keep their Beaufighters, Hurricanes, and Spitfires in combat readiness.

Though there were obviously several major and minor engine oil and hydraulic system leaks needing to be fixed prior to departure, a time consuming situation that couldn't be helped, the immediate need was to keep the monkeys from cooking in an airplane rapidly turning into a giant oven.

In true Bat Marlow style genius, came an arrangement of a series of electric fans to blow air through hemp matting that was kept wet by letting water trickle down the upwind side, thereby creating a "swamp cooler" type air conditioning system. This simple but ingenious method was learned by Bat in North Africa during the war when he observed the process being performed on a very hot day in the Libyan city of Benghazi. In that situation long ago, but still firmly etched into Bat's memory, a group of young Libyan boys were pouring sea water on large hemp sacks that were tied to a line hanging in front of a private dwelling's outdoor sitting area. The hot desert wind blowing through that wet hemp cloth produced remarkably cool air as it passed through, leaving Bat never to forget his introduction to air conditioning, desert style.

To repair the oil leaks they had to wait until night brought temperatures down enough to be able to work on the hot airplane. Meanwhile all energies went into keeping the cabin of the airplane cool enough for the monkeys to survive the terribly high heat of a standard summer day in Abadan, Iran.

By the time the Herjolffson brothers were ready to head out for Amsterdam everyone connected with the oil companies flight operation, including office clerks, pilots, even the air service's Director General, had participated in one way or another to help Jammie and Banjo out of their nightmare.

Just prior to departure, as they were preparing to pay the last of their finances to cover the fuel cost, Director General, Harry Hampton handed Jammie an envelope and said: "This is a little assistance from all of us here...and don't concern yourselves about the fuel, we aren't going to miss it." As Harry spoke those last words he turned and nodded his head toward the giant oil refinery on the eastern edge of Abadan, and then gave the brothers a huge smile.

Though Jammie did expect some help from Bat, just as the brothers would have given him, had the situation been reversed, this degree of generosity was wholly unexpected. The brothers had discussed and agonized over the problem of how they were going to pay for all the emergency services that the Abadan stop evolved into and decided on asking for time enough to deliver and sell the monkeys to clear their indebtedness.

They mentioned this to Bat shortly after realizing the enormity of the problems facing them prior to continuation of the trip, to his reply: "You bloody yanks, especially you two sorry sacks, come in here with a couple minor problems then start worrying your pretty heads about money...Bugger all, if that isn't just dandy...You quit that soft life on the farm to give us a hand with the bloody fucking Jerries, stuck with us to the end of the bleakness...and now you want to muck up my chance to say thank you?" Bat said in mock indignation.

"That was different...everybody had to chip in...besides, Banjo and I would never have escaped that damned farm... or rather, the **lovely** farm that paid for this C-46 and those monkeys...so you did us a favor...no, we got free flying lessons, food, and lodging for years from the RCAF...this here is another story. We owe you and your folks here, and we expect to pay you back...Bat, you're savin' our ass, we know it, and we intend to pay...soon as we can," Jammie said in all sincerity.

"I'll take up the matter with his holiness, Harry 'bloody' Hampton," Bat said, then expressed some displeasure at the thought.

Though the brothers wanted to depart for Amsterdam with as little fanfare as possible, it was not to be. It seemed that half the population of Abadan was there as they cranked up the old R2800s and waved goodbye to those kind and generous folks who hadn't wanted to miss witnessing the departure of the Herjolfsson brothers, and '**family**'.

It was a little past five a.m. when they got airborne, the air temperature a **'cool'** eighty something degrees. Cool, that is, compared to the dreadful daytime 140+ temps they'd been struggling to get through during the past several days strenuous efforts to save their monkeys from Abadan's deadly heat.

After a very pleasant eight hours and forty three minute flight via Basra, Iraq - Damascus, Syria - Beirut, Lebanon, they landed without incident in Athens to refuel, feed and water the monkeys, and grab a quick lunch in the passenger air terminal restaurant. The plane had performed flawlessly and upon a post flight "walk-around inspection", no oil leaks or discrepancies could be found.

"Jammie, if it hadn't been for your buddy, Bat Marlow, and that unbelievable out pouring of goodwill from all those people in Abadan, how in heck would we have ever been able to make it this far in our little junket?" Banjo said this as they climbed aboard the plane to close one more segment in their attempt to achieve a good and worthy life for themselves.

"If for no other reason, little brother, we've got to pull this thing off successfully in tribute to Julia....and Bat.... and there's all the other good folks who gave, right from their hearts, just to help us along the way." Jammie said in a solemn tone.

Four

IT WAS foggy at Amsterdam's " Schiphol International Airport", with a ragged ceiling of 300 feet and one mile visibility. A less than ideal situation considering that the plane's flight instruments hadn't been calibrated or, for that matter, ever been out of the instrument panel for many years.

Fortunately, Schiphol is fully equipped with advanced radar, electronic runway guidance systems, and airport lighting to guide aircraft down safely even under weather conditions where the ceiling and visibility are nil.

Banjo's superb talents for precision instrument flight gave Jammie no reason for concern about the instrument approach and landing. After passing over the "outer marker", locked onto the ILS Localizer center line, and starting down the "Glide Path", Schiphol tower gave them their final landing clearance for runway 23.

As they broke through the fog at about 350 feet above the ground, Jammie called out, "**minimums, and I've got the centerline lights, Banjo!!!**"

"O K, I've got the runway," Banjo said in a tone of voice totally void of emotion.

On touch down as the tires made contact with the pavement, there was a slight lurch toward the left accompanied by a definite metallic thud that resonated throughout the airframe. Banjo, though startled at this abnormal set of circumstances, instantly shoved in some right rudder and brake to correct for the airplane's tendency to drift toward the left side of the runway, a situation rapidly turning ugly. The plane was not responding to Banjo's efforts to regain directional control, frustrations which had reached the point where he decided there was no other alternative but to apply maximum power and get the plane into the air.

"Max power Jammie...I'm going to get us back into the air...something's haywire as hell!"

Without question Jammie adjusted the throttles for maximum engine power while also monitoring the critical engine instruments. As he routinely went about the tasks required of copilot duty on a C-46, he couldn't help wondering what this turn of events was going to lead to.

As both brothers concentrated intently to their immediate challenges salvaging a balked landing, one they both realized was considerably beyond a routine landing glitch, the plane suddenly slammed down to the left, followed instantly by an enormous crashing sound, a strong lurch to the left, they were jolted up against their seat belt restraints, then thrown down hard toward the right as the horrendous sounds of screeching metal being torn from the C-46 as it careened off the runway.

Throughout these dreadful moments of sheer terror, while both brothers were being banged helplessly about in their seats, Jammie suddenly experienced an overpowering transcendence of thought that seemed to overshadow all the din and horror of the moment. What his brain had perceived in that flash of time was their C-46 crying out wildly in her throes of dying agony, and to he heard his brother yell out at the top of his lungs : "**Ooooh shit!**" (Often a pilot's last vocal response to a nasty situation he has no control over, and which he has perceived probably be the final fall of the curtain)

Finally skidding, banging, and jolting heavily to rest somewhere on the airport's midfield turf, the plane lay tilted at a forty-five degree angle on her left side. Banjo finally caught his breath, and said: "How's that for an arrival, bro?"

Due to a newly developing sound reverberating loudly and frantic from the cabin of the plane, that of the terrified monkeys, Jammie couldn't make out what Banjo had said, so he asked him to repeat it.

"Seems like I'm a little rusty on my landing technique, or else we musta run over an elephant or somethin', bro!?" He said this with a chuckle, almost as if it wasn't any kind of a big deal.

Jammie, thankful that they were still alive and apparently not seriously injured, but far from feeling a like-sense of humor, replied: "I think we might best delve into it once we've extracted our butts from this thing, and before it torches!"

In the process of trying to escape being trapped in a burning airplane, a most terrorizing thought to anyone who has witnessed aviation high octane gasolines highly volatile nature when ignited, the brothers were startled to find themselves having to queue up behind a mob of highly agitated monkeys scrambling, squabbling, and all of them frantically trying to get out of the plane at the same time through a small mid cabin emergency escape hatch, that had apparently opened at some point during the crash.

Jammie and Banjo, in somewhat of a daze just stood mesmerized throughout the monkey evacuation drill. Every one of the bamboo cages had failed to survive the crash, though it appeared there were no serious casualties amongst the monkeys.

By the time the brothers had gotten out of the airplane and clear of the gasoline soaked turf, nary a monkey could be seen or heard . They had scattered to the four winds.

It had been a good three or four minutes since the plane had come to rest, the brothers were now sitting on the ground facing the remains of what had been their hoped for dreams of a good life. Neither spoke while lost in their private thoughts as they awaited the arrival of airport authorities. Not able to hold in his deep despair any longer, Banjo, in a subdued tone of voice, was saying to his brother, "**I kinda wish I'd died in the crash**," when no sooner the words were out of his mouth there was a very loud **'varooomp'** sound accompanied by a searing flash of great heat and brilliant light. The gasoline had finally ignited, and Banjo took it as an awakening to the horror of how it might have been had he been given his wish. It was as if God had been listening and decided it was time to step in for a scolding with heavy emphasis toward spectacular dramatization.

"You know, Banjo, I'm glad the old girl is going out in a blaze of glory...it kinda does

something toward emphasizing the facts of life...how it is when its something really good you're reaching out for, and it's so damned hard to latch onto...This is one of those things, and I feel real strong about it....We're on the right track, you mark my word, this is just another little setback!"

"Sounds like you bumped your head real bad, Bro." Banjo said with a chuckle, as they sat there watching their "little setback" go up in menacingly black smoke and angry flame.

The debris path was like looking at a long and narrow grave yard. Broken, twisted, and horribly mangled parts of what had been an elegantly proportioned airplane lay like tomb stones. A hot and hissing engine, its propeller still attached, lay there as if whimpering over the sadness of it all. Just up this pathway of gloom and doom, at the very beginning of the debris field, lay the culprit of this disaster. It stood out in such a way as to leave absolutely no doubt over the direct cause of this horrible holocaust.

The left landing gear tire had either gone flat during flight or immediately on contact with the runway at touchdown, and rather than allow the wheel to rotate, the great mass of tire and inner tube tended to pile up and wedge itself between the landing gear strut and wheel assembly. The chain of events that apparently followed were: The left landing gear strut failed, broke away, and allowed the plane to drop toward the left enough for the left wing tip and propeller to strike the runway. Because the engine had been developing full power at the instant the propeller struck the ground the combination of those forces caused the entire power plant assembly to tear itself free of the airframe structure, followed by the wildly gyrating engine and propeller assembly being overrun by the momentum of the out of control airplane.

"Banjo, when the engine came off, we slid right over it, and I guess that's what it was that tore the whole left wing off... including what fuel was left in the left tanks...that's probably what gave us time to get out...before she torched, I mean!"

"Yea, and it doesn't take any great amount of genius to realize we fucked up in assuming those old tires were OK... or was it that we were so damned hot-to-trot our judgement went haywire as hell?" Banjo said in a tone filled with self recrimination.

A couple hours later, after being released from the airport emergency medical clinic

with a clean bill of health, the brothers were seated in the airport director's conference room. A hearing was being held among the many officials about responsiblity for removal of the crash debris, and the rounding up and disposition of the monkeys. Beside collection, housing, and feeding the animals, public health issues pertaining to the possible spread of disease was causing considerable alarm and tension.

After about half an hour of listening to the sometimes highly emotional outbursts between the various officials, while both brothers were filing accident reports, signing numerous documents (all printed in Dutch), a heated argument broke out between the chief inspector of the accident investigation team and the airport director. The boiling point had been reached over a debris removal issue. The airport director wanted the debris removed immediately in order to restore use of the now closed runway. This was contrary to the demands of Chief Inspector / Dutch Civil Aviation Authority, who didn't want anything touched until his accident investigation inspectors had completed their official site investigation into probable cause for the accident.

While this highly dramatic scenario was taking place, neither side giving way to the other, remarks and accusations flying throughout the squabble over who was to **"pay for this, that, and the other thing"** Jammie suddenly realized that the crash and loss of their plane and all was merely the beginning of their nightmare. Like a drowning person desperate to save himself, an idea popped into his dome that might work, and though it was highly risky, it was either take a shot at it or suffer the total consequences of the financial liability aspects beginning to take shape before his eyes. Airfield cleanup costs, the monkey problem, costs involved in lost revenue to the airport and the airline companies, fines, endless claims were certain to plague them for years to come.

There was only one way out. Without a word of his intentions to Banjo, Jammie whispered to the airport directors assistant that he needed to make a phone call, that it was urgent. His request granted, Jammie spoke quietly to his brother to follow him and both slipped unobtrusively out of that noisy room full of bickering people. Jammie held his breath as they made there way toward the stairway leading down and into the busy airline passenger terminal area. His primary plan was simply to get into a taxi and get headed for downtown Amsterdam, to lose themselves in the city until they could put an escape plan together.

Five

THE TAXI delivered them to a downtown hotel the driver recommended as "most suitable" for American tourists. The only luggage they were carrying was a briefcase holding the airplane purchase documents and some of the plane's historical records. And, naturally, Banjo managed to come through the ordeal with his banjo intact. All other personal gear went up in smoke.

Checking into the temporary sanctuary of their hotel room they wasted no time in discussing their options. It was obvious they had to get out of Holland as fast as possible and because the train station was within easy walking distance, agreement was quickly reached on an initial plan of action that suggested they depart the hotel immediately, not bothering to check out, high-tail it to the train station, and buy tickets on the first train southbound out of Amsterdam.

At the ticket counter they were elated to learn there was a southbound train soon to depart for Liege, Belgium.

Arriving in Liege they changed to a bus for Luxembourg, trying to get as much distance between themselves and Amsterdam's nightmarish airport scene as quickly and furtively as possible.

As Jammie summed up his take on their plight, trying to rationalize their need for running from a further compounding of their disaster, he told Banjo they would make restitution for damages caused as soon as they were able: "It may take years, Banjo, but we will fix that, somehow, somewhere down the road, and that's a promise were going to keep!"

Stepping off the bus in Luxembourg Banjo made a beeline for a phone booth to look up the number of an airline company that an old friend of his was flying for, a Czechoslovakian pilot he had buddied around with during the bygone days of WW II, a time when they were assigned to an RAF bomber squadron flying the "Wellington", or "Wimpy", as the famous old plane was affectionately referred to by the men who flew in them.

The airline switchboard operator put Banjo through to their 'Manager of Flying Operations'. After using the World War Two "old buddy" routine, Banjo managed to learn his friend lived at the hotel located above the "**Good Times Bar**" in downtown Luxembourg, right in the center of town.

"**Good Times Bar**", Banjo was repeating as he looked at his brother while coming out of the phone booth, a pronounced quizzical expression on his face and in the tone of voice.

"What the hell are you talking about?...Any bar sounds like good times to me right about now...let's go!" Jammie said , adding a chuckle to his remark.

"No, Jammie, that name rings a bell....I mean, yes to your,' let's go', but an emphatic **'NO'** to your "any bar" remark...If my memory serves me correctly this particular bar belongs to a famous member of the "under ground", you know, those guys and gals who saved hundreds of shot down flyers from capture by the Germans during the war...I don't remember his name, but that "Good Times Bar" thing sure has jogged my memory…so, what do you say we get our butts on over there, and check the place out, big brother!?"

When Banjo asked the bartender how to go about renting a room in the hotel he was directed to a flight of stairs leading to the hotel's combined lobby and dining room on the floor directly above the bar.

Signing the hotel register they were informed by the concierge, a quite elderly man horribly stooped over, but with a kindly personality, whose heavily wrinkled dark face reminded one of prunes, that the rooms were rented by the month only. Payment to be in advance.

The "**month only**" and "**payment in advance**" words coming out of the concierge's mouth created a very disheartening effect on the brothers. What made it even more unsettling was the moment they had arrived at the place a feeling of being at home seemed to have come over them. The lobby and adjoining dining room were both filled with men of around their own age, all seemingly happy and boisterous in their gleeful conversations with one another. They were quite obviously all airmen, all excitedly rambling on with aviation terms in English, the international aviation language. Some spoke with heavily accented English and there were a number of Americans talking in a mixed bag of accents.

This was definitely where they belonged, at least for the time being, until they had figured a way out of their current predicament.

They decided to ask the concierge if they could meet with the hotel owner to discuss an important matter. Without any hesitation at all the brothers were surprised to be escorted to "Monsieur Antoine Xavier's" private office door, which the concierge merely tapped lightly, opened and escorted the Herjolfsson's into what turned out to be a nicely furnished apartment, the owners living quarters and apparently his business office.

Monsieur Xavier, standing in the middle of the sitting room as they entered, greeted them politely, offered his hand to both brothers, then asked them to be seated offering coffee or tea.

Antoine Xavier, though rather small of stature, was strikingly handsome with his full head of immaculately groomed white hair and debonairly stylish mustache. The way he was dressed you would think he was prepared to meet the Queen of England. This guy had an aura about him that certainly set him apart from ordinary men. It was quite easy to visualize him as one of those courageous people of WW II's "Netherlands Underground Brigade", the brave men and women whose daring exploits to save allied airmen from capture and imprisonment by the Nazi's will always be legend.

Antoine's handshake said a lot about the man. It was neither vice-grip nor dead fishlike, just a plain old firm and sincere hand shake, but somehow there was more to it that suggested here was real strength of character, something of a window into this good man's soul.

In near perfect English, Antoine said: "You are Americans, flyers looking for work I believe!...There is perhaps some kind of temporary paradox connected with your personal finances you wish to discuss with me, and do I sense something of a darker nature to your state of affairs, as well?"

Jammie and Banjo looked at each other with expressions of amazement on their faces.

"How did you know this, sir?" Jammie asked, his expression now indicating his amusement at Antoine's accurate summing up of their situation.

"I regret being so blunt, gentlemen, please forgive me!... It is in your faces...your manner...I meet many like you. Our world, is it not, a troublesome place in these times of great change!?...The challenges of daily life are many."

"Sir, we're way over our heads in, as you say; this **'troublesome place'!"** Banjo said with a forced smile.

"Please, how may I be of assistance to you gentlemen?" Antoine asked in a way showing genuine compassion.

This was the key for the brothers to open up to a man who appeared willing and able to come to their aid. They unloaded their whole story, even going back to the years of floundering around with their lives after the war, how Aunt Julia had been the actual motivational force behind the project at the outset. They told Antoine of the out-pouring of generosity from all those good folks in Abadan. When the telling of their story of woe got to Jammie's animated description of the crash itself, their escape from the plane after the last of the monkeys had passed through the escape hatch, how the monkeys were yelling their heads off as they scattered in all directions shortly before the plane exploded in flame, Antoine suddenly burst out laughing so heartily tears began flowing down his cheeks.

"Please excuse me gentlemen for my shameful performance! This story...your story...this real life troublesome happening of yours brings to mind the great cinema performers; 'Oliver and Hardy', I believe this to be true!"

"That's us alright...just a couple of clowns, but Auntie Julia isn't going to see it that way, unfortunately." Jammie said with straight face.

"Yes, I must admit, you are in a bit of a flap in this instance." Antoine stated flatly.

"Monsieur Xavier, sir, we are down on our luck to the point we've got enough cash to pay for a room for maybe a week, and that's going to leave us short of eating money, so I guess what I'm asking is....could you possibly use a couple of floor sweepers or dishwashers, or some kind of work we could trade you for meals until we can get ourselves squared away?" Banjo asked in a very subdued tone.

At that, Antoine arose from his chair, walked over to the brothers, turned them toward the door, and with his hands upon their shoulders, Antoine between the two of them, said: "Gentlemen, you Jammie, you Banjo, are my personal guests.

Your stay here is on my account....For your brave work in our fight against the Germans, and helping us of the resistance forces, it is my pleasure...my duty to be of service to you now.... Now, let us adjourn to the dinner table....I trust you could handle a bit of 'grub', as you Americans call it?"

"Antoine, sir, we want you to know we will accept your extremely kind offer, your generosity, only if you will allow us to pay you back when we find work, and in the meantime we want to be useful to you now in whatever way we can," Jammie said.

"Nonsense!...Please, you are my guests...I insist!" Antoine said this in a tone suggesting he would be offended if pressed on the issue.

Jammie now changed tactics: "Antoine, my brother is a very talented musician, a banjo playing wizard, would you like to hear him play?"

"Would you be so kind, Banjo?...the family, I am certain, will be most happy." Antoine said showing his excited anticipation.

"Nothing would make me feel better than to get my old banjo jumping with joy, in fact, sir, I'd like to play for the audience at the bar", Banjo said happily.

The brothers now feeling relieved to have at least one problem solved for the moment were soon to start getting acquainted with the other tenants of Antoine's hotel, most of whom were flight and ground crew men employed with one or another of Luxembourg's freelance aviation enterprises. Luxembourg International Airport, since shortly after the war, had been a beehive of activities due to it's free port type of operational status. Numerous entrepreneurial air carriers, small outfits, some with only one to three plane fleets performed in charter and contract cargo operations on a world wide basis.

It was good for Luxembourg's economy and a real boon to the international gathering of small airline companies who enjoyed a wide range of operational freedoms nonexistent anywhere else in the entire western world. Luxembourg was a true haven to aviation's disenfranchised, greatly influencing the city/country to becoming the wonderfully refreshing international flavor it enjoys to this day.

Within a couple of weeks of Banjo's musical talent and Jammie's card playing, they had earned enough money to pay Antoine for their board and room, which he refused to accept until they had landed regular jobs.

In the middle of their third week, as Antoine's "**guests**" at his "Good Times Bar and Hotel", things took a major turn toward the positive; they both got hired on with "**High Seas Airline**", one of the larger of the Luxembourg based carriers, with a fleet of several C-46 and DC-4 types of planes.

High Seas Airline was one of the more aggressive outfits, plying it's trade mostly in charter work between Europe and Africa, hauling guns, ammunition, and all sorts of military equipment to one side or the other, occasionally both, of the multitudes of warring factions fighting one another for control over that great myriad of Europe's ex African colonies.

Each of these small, now newly independent nations, were an excellent source of business for the small, and totally independent, air carriers doing business out of Luxembourg, and Belgium. Business was flourishing for this band of aviation brothers, so much so that Banjo and Jammie were to find themselves on their way to Africa within a matter of days after signing on with High Seas.

They were put through an accelerated ground school program consisting of key (in some cases highly critical) subjects specific to this unique type of airline operation: Coverage in company policy, international air law, and an excellent C-46 equipment refresher. This was immediately followed by a one hour practice session of flight maneuvers in preparation for passing a check ride given by High Seas owner, general manager, ground school instructor, flight instructor, chief pilot, and flight examiner. Though he was a guy who wore many hats, worked practically around the clock, he showed no outward signs of fatigue or stress. An impressive airman to say the very least, and to Banjo and Jammie, an example of what they would like to have become, had their luck not gone so awfully awry on that infamous day in Amsterdam.

Six

WITHIN A mere few days since signing on with High Seas Airline, passing check rides, being fitted for and receiving their uniforms, they were off to a destination in Africa neither had ever heard of previously, a place called "Usumbura", the capital city of a country called "Urundi" located in east-central Africa.

The trip to Usumbura, located near the northern shores of Lake Tanganyika, involved the delivery of a twenty thousand pound load of assorted weapons and ammunition originally intended to be flown in one of the airlines' four engine DC-4s . However, the DC-4 was grounded at Fort Lamy, Chad, with engine trouble while on it's return from a previous trip to Usumbura.. To meet the delivery schedule for this large load, with no other DC-4s readily available, two C-46s were being substituted to carry the load. Though a C-46 can carry 10,000 pounds of pay load, even more, the great distances between North Africa's refueling places along this route, the most direct and shortest, dictated considerably more fuel was required for the trip. In this instance the 10,000 pound payload put the plane approximately 2,000 pounds over the maximum allowable gross takeoff weight. **"Allowable"**, in this case, refers to the limiting criteria for the C-46 airplane were it being operated under US certification rules, but not necessarily so under operational authority within foreign airline operations where aviation safety standards are often quite different from those of North America's.

Under the operating rules Jammie and Banjo were governed by in their new flying job they were "legal" to make this trip. **"Legal"** according to the air laws of Luxumbourg at the time. This does not mean the C-46 would handle as well with an engine failure on takeoff (or enroute) while carrying those extra 2,000 pounds above and beyond weight and balance limits established in accord with America's very high safety standards of the time. US Civil Aviation Administration engineers developed civil airline operating limitations for the C-46 by working in consort with Curtiss-Wright, the manufacturer of the airplane, ultimately leading to its certification for US commercial operations.

Another set of airplane operating standards, those for military cargo and troop transport aircraft originally designed and built specifically for military use, often allowed for considerably more payload to be carried, and commensurably the lesser degree of operational safety. Under military "**wartime-emergency**" flight operations an additional escalation in allowable departures from standard operating limits could come into play. A good example of this occurred in the Korean War when pilots in the US Air Force 21st Troop Carrier Squadron, (of which this author was one of the pilots) often were loaded without any regard for limitations per "Airplane Flight Manual". Our C-47s (military version of the DC-3) were loaded to what ever was considered possible to stagger into the air, and on many occasions we made takeoffs at gross weights as high as 34,000 pounds.

To give that number some credence, the same airplane in civilian airline use in USA was limited to a maximum takeoff gross weight of 25,200 pounds. This whole situation revolved around the degree of flying safety standards the particular governing authority would deem acceptable in event of an engine failure.

The two C-46s were duly loaded and lifted off for **'deep dark'** Africa. A crew well experienced in these shadowy arms operations, and taking the lead, was captained by a German national (ex WW II Luftwaffe pilot), his copilot a young Britisher.

The trip proceeded without a hitch until an engine failed on the lead plane about one hundred miles west of the rugged 14,000 to 16,000 foot high Mitumba mountain range. It couldn't have happened at a worse place along the route. Stanleyville, in the Congo, the only alternate airport west of the Mitumba range was 300 miles behind them, too far for the very high fuel consumption rate of single engine operation under conditions that required maximum available horsepower (and correspondingly huge fuel flow) merely to try minimizing their altitude drift-down. Their only option was to continue eastward toward Usumbura and hope for enough altitude to cross over the Mitumba's, or find a pass.

Their luck ran out when visibility became obscured upon entering a dense cloud condition formed by moist jungle air flowing up-slope into the cooler atmosphere over foothills of the Mitumba Range. They were at an altitude too low to clear the high ground and apparently unable to see well enough through the clouds to find a pathway through a pass. The final radio call from the crew was the copilot's voice: "I don't think we will make...." Though the brothers made numerous radio calls attempting to contact them, hoping desperately to hear a reply, it just wasn't going to happen. Somewhere in those terribly rugged and remote mountains is the final resting place of a stalwart aircrew, a Curtiss C-46, and 10,000 pounds of war goods that aren't going to cause harm to anyone.... I guess that's the only thing good about this facet of the story...

When Jammie and Banjo landed in Usumbura and the Urundi authorities learned only half of their shipment had arrived they refused to believe the brothers explanation. They chose, rather, to assume they had been cheated by the **"European devils"**. No matter how hard the brothers tried they couldn't get the government agent assigned to receive the shipment (an army colonel who happened to be elaborately decked out in full dress uniform and carrying a swagger stick and all number of medals upon his tunic) to understand that the 20,000 pounds originally to be coming by DC-4 had been placed on two C-46s, and that the other C-46, carrying the other half of the load, had crashed in the Congo. The colonel's refusal to believe the Herjolfsson brothers was backed by the fact Urundi had been victimized by another **"short shipment"** problem in the recent past. To the colonel's way of looking at the situation and by adding some African Independent Nation **logic**, the simple solution to the problem was to offer the brothers, Jammie and Banjo Herjolfsson, free lodging in Usumbura's 'finest' hotel until that undelivered part of the shipment arrived in **"good and proper order"**.

"Holy suffering katzenjammers, Jammie!...How in hell are we getting out of this one, big brother?" Banjo said, in a dismal tone of voice, as they were being escorted to Usumbura's 'finest' hotel.

"We've had more than enough practice to handle situations bordering along lines that appear disastrous at the outset....This is really nothing in comparison to dear old Amsterdam!...Now, is it, Banjo?"

"When you put it that way...I suppose you're right, but remind me again when they lead us out to one of those great big vats of boiling water...like they used show in those old African movies...remember em, Jammie!?"

"Ha ha ha!...right, Banjo, but they're not going to revert back to that kind of stuff. These people are supposedly civilized now...Heck, they've had years and years under colonial rule...I think it was Germany first, and now it's the Belgians running the show, so I wouldn't worry too much about the big boiling pot you're fixated on."

After nearly three weeks of solitary confinement in Usumbura's finest hotel, in reality a world class "**roachatorium**", the brothers found themselves in a real-time hell on earth. Unrelenting equatorial heat combined with humidity so high the brothers felt as if drowning in their own sweat, and though feeling absolutely physically and mentally drained, Jammie's sense of humor suddenly kicked in: "Banjo!...I was wrong, you had it right, we're actually being boiled in our own fat!"

The combined negatives of it all, the terrible food, constant diarrhea, the nagging uncertainties of what, if anything, the airline company was doing about their situation, would they be hauled out and put before a firing squad? Living under the weight of all this was starting to take it's toll. Had it not been for their superior strengths of character and an inordinately strong brotherly support for one another at the occasional '**downs**' in composure, the ordeal would have been considerably less tolerable.

Then one morning, right out of the blue, no warning, fanfare, or explanation of any kind, they were escorted to a ramshackle bus by the illustrious colonel, told to board and never to return to Urundi...ever again!

The bus trip seemed like torture by thrashing machine, but at least they were heading away from the solitary confinement of that sweat box like hotel in 'lovely downtown Usumbura', Urundi. Where they were going, when they would arrive, and any other questions weren't worth considering...they were being resurrected from hell and that's all that mattered...for the time being, at least.

Though totally exhausted by the time their hot, over crowded, stench filled, extremely noisy, and rough riding bus arrived in Kigali, capital of neighboring Ruanda, the brothers were rudely herded, with twenty of their busmates and some others picked up in Kigali, all blacks, to an ancient Flatbed type truck minus it's side racks, and told in no uncertain terms to climb aboard.

As it turned out the bus ride had seemed almost luxurious in comparison to this considerably less comfortable conveyance as they now lurched, jerked, and bounced their way out of extremely hot and dusty Kigali heading in a general northern direction to a destination of no return.

Like Jammie and Banjo, their colleagues it seems were also undesirables being dispossessed like so much garbage. Amongst these sorrowful looking simple souls there was great interest in the odd shaped case Banjo was carrying so protectively. In time, their curiosity getting the best of them, they just had to know what was inside that mysterious case.

The way the brothers were dispatched from Usumbura, and again in Kigali, they had no opportunity to take anything in the way of food or water with them, and it wasn't looking favorable for their hunger and thirst pangs to disappear anytime soon until Banjo suddenly realized he might have a powerful bargaining chip for some of the luscious looking fruit their companions were pulling out of bags.

Finally giving in to any semblance of pride or self consciousness Banjo opened the mysterious shiny black case, pulled out his beloved banjo and with hand gestures managed to get his point across: "**Music for food**".

From that point on in this leg of their wild and wooly odyssey, for mile after bouncing, swerving, joggling mile, that truckload of destitutes turned into a musical concert on wheels, the likes of which Africa was probably never to witness again.

Everyone joined in accompaniment to Banjo's wonderfully melodious and lively repertory of his favored selections of old, tried and true, "**Blue Grass**". Country music at it's absolute best. Everybody, man woman and child, hummed and swayed to the rhythm of that magical music in perfect unison. Banjo, being in his perfect element, couldn't help but completely forget about the problems that were certain to lay ahead. It was a case for: "Live for the moment , for who knows what should await our fate!"

Even the two police escorts in the cab of the truck could be seen enjoying the magic of Banjo's true calling.

At a pause between songs Jammie remarked to his brother, "I wonder what Aunt Julia would think if she saw how well we fit into this scene here....with all these minstrels of your traveling road show on wheels...here we are in the middle of deep dark Africa, sandwiched in with all these poor buggers on this dilapidated old flat bed wreck just singing at the top of our lungs, all fat dumb and hilariously happy....what do you think, Banjo?"

"Oh my God, Jammie, why did you have to bring Aunt Julia into this?...But now that I'm thinking about it, you know, all that money from selling the farm....the beautiful hopes and plans and prayers....everything's boiled down to us sitting here with these simple soulmates of ours, like on a journey that God hasn't quite gotten around to deciding on our destiny... Seems like this whole damned scenario is some kinda test.... like maybe he's got something grand planned for us on down the road.... if we can prove our worth...and I gotta admit, I'm gettin a bit tired of the suspense if that's how it's supposed to play out."

It was in the middle of "Red River Valley",one of Banjo's favorite songs , when the truck came to a jolting stop just short of a bridge spanning a rather large river. One of the two Ruanda policemen then bellowed in an ugly tone of voice to get off the truck. He gave the order in a number of

African dialects common to the area.(Undoubtedly included would have been; Bantu, Kinyarwanda, Kiswahili, Hamitic, and Swahili in a Tanganyika dialect.) Most surprising was his quite reasonable facsimile of **English** in the clipped style spoken by British military officers.

Once everyone had gotten off the truck, their possessions of a lifetime strapped to their backs, or being carried in a variety of rolled-up canvas's, burlap sacks, and the like, the vocal officer in charge pointed to the north and said, "Kagatumba, Uganda is on other side of Kagera" (the river forming the Ruanda and Uganda border) "People want to go Uganda, cross bridge!" Then he looked directly at the Herjolfsson brothers, and in what they interpreted as an order, more or less, he pointed to the river and said , "Go down Kagera to Kyaka, take road to Bukoba, take steamer!"

That said, the policemen boarded the truck, hurriedly turned it around, and in their great haste to head South and remove themselves from this scene of destitute and rejected people, spun the truck's wheels sufficiently to create one hell of an enormous cloud of onerous and suffocating red dust.

Most of the group started trudging across the bridge, their faces indicating the depth of sadness and despair they felt from rejection, and to the unknowns of a destiny that lay in store for them in, yet, just another turmoil ravaged country.

"Lord almighty, what'd we do to end up in the God awful wilds of Africa like this, Banjo?"

"Seems the good Lord 'hath' chosen this way, Jammie old buddy... I guess he's say'in, 'get your shit together, young fellas!' "

They were in a quandary on which way to start walking. With no map or even any basic knowledge of the area where they had been dumped was bad enough, now that nightfall was descending upon them as well had the effect that put them into a state where full survival mode took over. As reality set in, hearts pumping pure adrenaline, the voice of an old man suddenly seemed to come from out of nowhere, "Come this way my friends!....Tanganyika is best way."

In the fading light of day Banjo spotted the old timer in the distant gloom signaling to follow him. Along the trail paralleling the river they went. The pace was quite fast. Some of the people, loaded down with their sole possessions, some with small children tagging along desperately trying to keep up, were showing signs of despair. Jammie and Banjo, basically unburdened with only their shared small suitcase and the Banjo case, each took it upon themselves to lend a helping hand where needed.

In what seemed a very long and burdensome time to keep up with their compatriots, the bunglesome loads, tripping over roots and stones in numerous rough places along, what had become, a pitch black trail, they came upon a beat-up old wharf. Tied up was an ancient steamer appropriately named, "Kagera Swan". The boat was about fifty feet in length with a fifteen foot beam and made from native hard wood. The first members of the group were buying passage and throwing their belongings aboard, and they were doing a lot of pushing and shoving to secure a comfortable spot on the foredeck of the old tub.

When Jammie's turn came to buy passage, the Captain, a rugged and very weathered looking white man in dirty khaki shorts, shirtless, a head of long white hair and full beard to match, spoke English with a heavy German accent too thick to accurately understand.   It took the old man, the one who had suggested they take the river route trail, to get things squared away. What it turned out the captain was asking of Jammie, was the "class" of travel they wanted . Would they want First Class accomodation, or would they settle for the open air of Kagera Swan's foredeck?

"First class" turned out to be a tiny cabin below decks furnished with two bunk beds on which lay highly stained straw ticked mattresses, a small porthole, and an almost overpowering aroma of vomit.

By the time the brothers entered their "First class" cabin they were so exhausted and weary they just collapsed on the wooden slats of their bunks, (after removing the stinking, and quite probably vermin filled mattresses), and slept like the dead.

The Kagera Swan remained tied to her berth overnight. At the crack of dawn, with a blast of her shrill whistle, Jammie and Banjo arose out of their slumber so quickly they both cracked their heads in the cramped quarters of "First Class" on the good ship, "Kagera Swan".

Ahead of the lot was a twelve hour journey down the Kagera to where the Bukoba - Musaka road crossing was, and where they would leave old Kagera Swan. The old African gentleman who had guided them thus far, who seemed to have something of an understanding of the brothers plight, suggested they follow his lead. They learned the kindly old fellow was going to Bukoba to buy passage on the Lake Victoria steamer for Kisumu where there was nearby rail connection for Nairobi. It was learned that the old fellow was going to live with his daughter and son-in-law in Nairobi. He was so happy in the telling of the story about going to live with his daughter he was nearly beside himself with joy.

The brothers knew Nairobi as a civilized and modern city. They didn't need any convincing from their traveling companion that it was Nairobi they must reach in order to wiggle their way out of their problem. The endless series of nightmares that had befallen them ever since the very beginning of the odyssey was beginning to wear heavily on their nerve ends.

The Kagera River trip turned out to be a 50% white knuckle and 50% stark death defying ordeal, leaving the brothers to wonder if this avocation might be the reason why the captain of the Kagera Swan's hair and beard had turned such a "snowy white".

At the Bukoba road terminus for Kagera Swan they rode the twenty odd miles to the city of Bukoba in a thirty passenger bus with at least sixty people in and atop the grossly overloaded vehicle. Jammie and Banjo, being novices in the art of taking public bus transportation in Africa had been too slow after departing the Swan to get seats inside the bus. Consequently, riding on top they enjoyed getting thoroughly soaked from a late afternoon cloud burst, but not until they had been thoroughly encrusted with reddish colored dust, the typical color of Africa's volcanic soil in that whole general area. Quite obviously, when red dust is mixed with water, one's coloring (skin, hair, clothing, and all) is going to follow suit.

"Banjo, did you know that you are beginning to look more like an African every day now, but with a pronounced reddish tinge to your dark coloring?" Jammie said with a chuckle.

"Big brother, did you know that the whites of your eyeballs and ivories are the only things separating you from the color of everything else around here?" Banjo countered, smiling broadly.

"Reminiscent of Al Jolson on the vaudeville stage and his portrayal of blackface minstrels, wouldn't you say?"..."In fact, if you were to start singing 'Mammy' while strumming away on yo' ole' banjo, I think it'd be mighty good for my morale right about now, little bro." Jammie said and they both got a good laugh out of that. Of course it never did take much persuasion to get Banjo to do his most favored thing, that of putting on a singing and banjo playing performance.

The bus rolled into Bukoba to the sound of loud and wonderfully melodious banjo music accompanied by the harmonious voices of everybody on the bus humming along with Banjo singing "**MAMMY**"at the top of his voice.

Seven

THEY HAD arrived in Bukoba on a Monday and learned the steamer "USOGA" would be departing for Kisumu, Kenya at 2230 (10:30 that night), a stroke of luck, otherwise they'd have to wait until the following Friday to catch the ship on it's return voyage, traveling in the opposite direction on it's standard scheduling of alternating from clockwise to counter-clockwise circuits around the lake.

After checking into the best hotel they could find, one in which their room was quite clean, had a ceiling fan that squeaked, and arrangements could be made for getting their clothes washed and iron dried, they took advantage of the clothes cleaning service. After a shower and shave, now dressed in their clean clothes they wandered downstairs to the hotel bar with an enormous thirst for a cold drink of something, anything cold and wet. What they had to settle for was a Tanganyika beer, brewed locally. Though anything but cold, it definitely was wet, **strong**, and so good tasting to the dry mouths of these two brothers they just couldn't seem to get enough of that delightful brew to adequately quench their thirst. You've got to picture these poor devils in that perpetually hot, humid, equatorial part of **"deep dark"** Africa, these two characters who hadn't been able to enjoy the simple little basics of life one gets accustomed to in the world of western civilization, for quite a dismal spell.

Before they knew what hit them a rather severe state of inebriation had descended upon the poor buggers. It was fortunate that the bartender took pity on them. Having overheard the two discussing their need for catching the USOGA that night, he mentioned the situation to the hotel manager who, in turn, assigned the hotel's concierge with the responsibility of escorting the two roaring drunks to their room to sleep off a bit of their "happy time at the bar", and the poor concierge was further charged with making certain that they would be on that "jolly good steam ship" USOGA when she sailed away.

Everything worked out reasonably well in the getting of the Herjolfsson boys "poured" onto the USOGA, but that isn't to suggest the boys were physically well. In fact, they were to learn about one of the hidden adversities to drinking that tasty Tanganyika beer in excessive quantities. To make matters worse, they were to experience this aboard a stinking, throbbing, rolling ship in the horribly suffocating heat of equatorial Africa. To endure a simple hangover is one thing any able-bodied aviator can handle with grace, if not a tiny bit of grimace, but Tanganyika beer would fall into a totally new dimension if one were to seek a specific classification scale of world class hangovers after tilting a few bottles of that liquid dynamite.

Several hours into the eight hour journey required to reach Mwanza, Tanganyika the two 'dashing cavaliers' were jarred awake to the sound of the ship's extremely loud horn shrieking out in the darkness. Instantly, almost like an echo, another ship's horn could be heard somewhere far out in that eerie blackness of night as the two steamers passed, one heading north west toward Bukoba and USOGA chugging and throbbing her way to the southern extremity of Lake Victoria. In statute miles this second largest lake on the planet is approximately 250 miles long and 150 miles wide. With an area of nearly 70,000 square miles the lake is so large it's almost like an inland sea. Right there in the middle of 'deep dark' Africa, at an elevation of 3,721 feet above sea level, our two vomit laden young aviators are lying flat on their backs on the foredeck of the grand old Lake Victoria steamer "USOGA". Unable to get back to sleep since the blasting of ships horns, they lay there amongst dozens of traveling companions, the gentle black denizens of the region. Staring up at the endless expanse of space, the awesome heavens above, Banjo looked over at his brother and said: "How in Gods little green acres is this wildly exotic life of ours going to turn out, Jammie?..... I mean, when is something with a reasonable degree of logic going to allow us a shot at it?"

"I've been laying here wondering the same thing, little bro.....I'm thinking it better show up before long cause we're running out of green backs....something like five hundred bucks is all that's remaining outa the airplane's emergency / contingencies fund, and Nairobi - if we ever manage to get there, is still one hell of a long way from anywhere."

"What makes it worse is having to make a career outa just getting to Nairobi. I mean like this boat ride....thirty two and a half hours to get to Kisumu, with all the ports of call we're going to be making, and then another fourteen hours on East African Railways old locomotive. Shit, we're going to be old and gray by the time we pull into Nairobi." Banjo said forlornly.

"Sure gives a guy perspective on what airplanes truly represent when you end up in a forced learning experience like the one we're in the middle of....wouldn't you say so, Banjo?"

"I wonder how and when we're going to get outa Nairobi, or is it going to be another case of being left to our wits, our overly strained intellect? Is it going to be another situation of back to square one and wriggle up up and away in our desperate search for better times?....Shit, Bro, I'm getting tired of all this down-trodden kinda crap all the fucking time." Banjo said in his way of letting off some steam from his pent up emotions.

"We'll handle everything that's thrown at us....just like always, and from everything I've ever heard about Nairobi through the years, it's not all that bad a place for pilots down on their luck....don't forget, that's where "Dambusters" is, you know, the bar that's something like the "Good Times Bar" back in Luxembourg." Jammie said in trying to take the ragged edge off their plight. Jammie was also suffering from all the turmoil they had been exposed to. Since the very start of the project, clear back to their arrival in India and getting ripped off throughout the purchase of the C-46, all the calamity that had plagued them ever since, would most definitely be enough to weaken the verve of anyone. Fortunately for the Herjolsson brothers, great strength of character was in their make up, and 'proof of the pudding' was that they were: "handling everything that had been thrown at them and coming back for more."

The steamer trip was pleasant enough once the hangovers gradually subsided, but that eight hour sail to Mwanza and four hour port stop, then after an eight and a half hour sail to Musoma and it's two hour port stop, there was yet another ten hour sail to reach port in Kisumu. It was just after seven o'clock Wednesday morning when they finally got off the steamer in Kisumu. Not wishing to prolong their stay a moment longer than necessary they made their way to East African Railway's train station without delay and bought second class tickets on the next train for Nairobi.(choosing second class tickets was decided in the interest of stretching their rapidly dwindling finances) The steam powered locomotive was to depart at 1945 (07:45 p.m.) that evening with an arrival in Nairobi scheduled for nine o'clock Thursday morning. This would put their knotty peregrinations right at seven days since departing the hotel at Usumbura, Urundi. The week of touring Africa, native style, with the living and feeling the oppressiveness of being the downtrodden, the dispossessed.

During the long and uncomfortable train ride, while suffering through a multitude of station stops all along way, the incessant heavy clattering of the wheels rolling across the rail segment joints, the coach jerking and rolling and creaking, the malodorous atmosphere from hot and sweating bodies jammed in the car like sardines, all combined with that irritating unknown: "What was to be in store for them at the end of this two hundred mile, fourteen hour (intensified) lesson in humility?"

It was somewhere along the way when Banjo murmured, as if to himself, in another little slip of melancholy: "When the money runs out.....what then?"

"**Easy!**...Dambusters will hire a Banjo player and I'll revert back to my old standbys; cards, pool, whatever the place runs in the way of games of chance....quit worrying about minor incidentals!....Everything's going to work out once we get to Nairobi, little brother, I can feel it in my bones...mark my word!"

Throughout the rest of the train ride they were able to relax and enjoy African scenery at it's best. Elephants, and all the marvelous wildlife one would hope to see on safari.

Eight

AFTER STEPPING down off the train in Nairobi it seemed almost as if they had miraculously been transposed to some quaint and beautifully manicured country village in England. There were multitudes of colorful shrubs, plants, bushes, and trees everywhere one looked.. It was simply a little bit of heaven with all the fragrance and color of floral gardens abounding the entirety of Nairobi. Highways and streets were lined with exquisite flowers, and to the immense delight of the Herjolfsson brothers those previous thoughts of dread simply disappeared as they made their way to city center and the luxuries of first rate hotel accommodations in this luscious little gem of **civilization.**

The dramatic change in place with so much of natures beauty to marvel at had an effect on one to drink it in gluttonously, and yet it was merely one of those soulful gifts of God's creations that placed a positive effect upon the hearts, and souls of Jammie and Banjo thereby re- instilling their courage and resolve to get back on track....somehow, and without delay.

After checking into a first class hotel, not even bothering to ask for room rates, Jammie got a telegraph cable off to their employer, "Seven Seas", in Luxembourg. Now all they had to do was relax in the comparative luxury of civilization, as it was in 1950's Nairobi, Kenya.

Jammie was almost certain he had an ex RAF Spitfire pilot buddy from WW II working for East African Airways, living here in Nairobi. Calling the airline's personnel office he asked for the pilot's phone number. The clerk informed him he had been working for East African until about a year and a half ago when he and his entire family had been killed by Mau Mau terrorists at the families farm. Jammie then mentioned to the clerk, who had appeared quite cordial on the phone, a bit about his and Banjo's background with the RCAF and their recent experience in Urundi and Ruanda.

"Oh my goodness!...Right, yes we have heard unconfirmed reports of your wildly flamboyant adventure...Ominous rumor has had it you were both executed a fortnight ago in Urundi... Fact is there is a big flap on at the UN about you chaps.... something about High Seas Airline flying munitions for the Commies as well as UN backed tribes in the Congo. Very clever indeed....By the by, would you and your brother like to join me and some of the other EAA chaps for a pint or two this afternoon?"

"Sounds like a great idea, sure would...Where and when do we meet?"

"Very good of you....Captain....Herjolfsson....Will fifteen hundred suit your pleasure, sir,...at Dambusters?"

"Dambusters? Jammie asked.

"Oh, right oh! At the aerodrome, you see!...Dambusters Aero Club is, I dare say, our **'rather'** principal watering hole, unofficial 'HQ' of RAF 617 Squadron, of bye gone times.... the old Lancaster unit that raised such proper havoc to Jerries

Ruhr river valley dams!....I do trust you recall 617 Squadron's significant contribution toward ending the great war, do I not!?" The man spoke in a forceful manner.

"You're sure right about that 'Lanc' outfit doing a good job throwing cold water on the Krauts...flooded all heck outa' the Ruhr....And, please, we're just plain **'Jammie',** and my brother's, **'Banjo'."**

Just prior to leaving the hotel for their afternoon social with the local aviation crowd at the Dambusters Banjo came out with: "Jammie,... now please don't accuse me of 'going around the bend', but I gotta level with you,...I'm beginning to wonder if the big guy upstairs isn't putting us through all this nutty crap for some great master plan he's got all worked out to see if we're qualified to hack it....you know, something grand and glorious....otherwise what's it all about?"

"Strange you should happen to bring that up cause I'm getting this recurring thought that we're sawing off the same damn limb we're sittin' on." Jammie said with a chuckle.

"Two superior minds tippy toeing off into the fading sunset, hand in hand, breathlessly awaiting word from God of their salvation to be!?" Banjo said sarcastically.

"Mockery isn't going to hack it one way or the other, Banjo. Let's just try hanging in there and see which way the ball bounces from here on out...OK, pal!?"

"Like we have any choice in the matter, bro?"

"Right, and we do have a choice. The choice of being men who can take one setback after another until the old worm turns the other way....and when it does we're gonna' handle the pluses good and proper!...It's gotta happen this way or else there's no rhyme nor reason to this thing they taught us about having faith in God!...Right?"

"When you put it that way I guess so, but you gotta admit it's getting close to time that damned worm of yours turns."

At Dambusters, to the great delight of both Herjolfsson's, they met a few ex-squadron mates, some others with mutual acquaintances of friends from the long gone past. It turned into a rousing good party among 'birds of a feather, all'. They started out being introduced to the large body of club members presented by their host, EAA's managing director of flying personnel, who told the brothers he hadn't seen that many members in attendance for a long time. He attributed this to a 'word-of-mouth' campaign throughout Nairobi's very active **'aviation grape vine'**, a miraculous and sudden appearance of the now, internationally famous "**lost airmen**" of the infamous High Seas Airline.

Jammie, caught up in this unexpected situation with such a highly charged atmosphere of good will, camaraderie, and high spirits began to realize a speech was in order, a word of appreciation and gratitude to these people for their outpouring of warmth and genuine concern for their well-being.

Putting his hands up to signify he had something to say to all present: "Gentlemen, I want you to know, and I'm speaking for my brother as well, it is sure good to be standing here amongst friends....birds of the feather, if you will. You people have touched our hearts with your kind words and concern for our well-being. The other two pilots of our two plane shipping consignment didn't fare as well as Banjo and I....They ran totally out of luck....their C-46 was limping on one engine, a night black as heck, then nearing the western slopes of the Mitumba Range they ran into a dense cloud condition..... I guess the only way you could put it is that the poor fellows just ran the gauntlet of their time on earth."

At this very moving point of the, up till now, gay and boisterous mood of the party, a definite hush descended upon the room. There was hardly a murmur to be heard. Learning the tragic fate of fellow airmen gave everyone present a moment of soul searching. The dampening effect seemed to linger on beyond a polite reverence toward the fallen pilots. Somewhat startled at the depth of emotion displayed and realizing something needed to occur to bring things out of the doldrums and back to the happy time intended, Banjo suddenly realized what it was going to take. Nudging his brother's arm and pointing to his banjo, Jammie instantly got the message.

"Gentlemen, my brother has sensed it is time for some of his real "down home blue grass", music like you folks may not have ever heard played by an aviator, but this guy can truly make his banjo talk."

Banjo quickly became the star attraction at Dambusters turning the party into one heck of a loud and joyous occasion that lasted until the wee hours. It was always like that when Banjo's magic fingers started plucking away. Every face in that club had changed from sadness to surprised looks of wonder and awe at the unbelievably melodious sounds they were now being treated to.

When the Herjolfsson brothers departed Dambusters for their hotel that morning they left with the knowledge they had a lot of new friends.

Late that afternoon after a restful sleep and during a hearty meal in the hotel restaurant a cable was hand delivered to them at their table. High Seas Airline, it turned out, no longer was in existence. The airline's owner had disappeared quite suddenly under quite mysterious circumstances according to the cable and whoever it was that sent the cable represented a mystery in itself.

"Now isn't that a dandy little ditty, eh Jammie!?"

"You know, Banjo, we seem to be operating on the backside of the power curve...like I wonder what it'd be like to run outta all this good luck we're having?"

"Well, I suppose bad luck is better'n no luck at all."

Back at Dambusters, the brothers got the word out to what had happened and asked for some help to get a ride northbound - anywhere heading north.

The following morning at 5:30 the phone woke the brothers out of a restless nights sleep: "This the notorious High Seas crew lookin for a ride ta the north?"

"That's us, friend....what's the good word?" Banjo said with a tired sounding and hoarse voice.

"Djibouti...you know, French Somaliland...I'm flyin a Gooney Bird for Air Djibouti...leavin about zero seven an a half...yuh need'n a lift, come on out to the airdrome!"

"Sure do, buddy. We'll be there, and what's your name?" Banjo said.

"Clark Harrington...everbody calls me Buster."

"OK Buster, we're on our way, thanks a lot." Banjo said as he shut the phone down on it's cradle, threw the covers off and scrambled out of bed.

They wasted no time checking out of the hotel and had no trouble circumventing the airport passenger terminal hassle by proceeding directly to the cargo terminal where Buster had directed them to go: "to minimize the usual boarding **crapola**", as he put it.

It was around seven fifteen when Jammie spotted a giant of a white man sauntering toward the cargo shed.. "This must be our hero heading this way, Banjo...I love his uniform... especially that 'New York Yankees' baseball cap...Jesus what a character we're about to be rescued by." It definitely was Buster, all six foot six, cowboy boots, and carrying a great big smile to match his girth and quite obviously happy-go-lucky nature.

"Hi fellas, Buster Harrington at your service." He said as he approached with his hand out.

"Sure good to meet another American, Buster...I'm Jammie Herjolfsson and this is my brother Bjarni, better known as 'Banjo'."

"It's good ta meet the famous High Seas crew alive an kicken...specially when the old rumor mill had ya'll tortured ta death in the Congo or somewheres like that."

"And we're mighty appreciative of you taking us along on your bird, Buster...thanks a lot." Banjo said.

They arrived in Mogadiscio, Somalia on schedule at eleven o'clock, had a leisurely two hour break for lunch while the DC-3 was being serviced with fuel and oil, the 'honey bucket' dumped, some cargo off loaded, and a few passengers and cargo added.

It was around five thirty that evening when they finally arrived in Djibouti, French Somaliland, after one hell of a turbulent ride across the Ogaden, a good part of the journey suffering through a cabin atmosphere heavily charged with sweating bodies and the putrid odor of vomit. It was that time of year on the Ogaden when surface temperatures can reach 150 degrees Fahrenheit (66 degrees C) at midday. Even though they were cruising at an altitude of eight thousand feet the cabin temperature must have been hovering around 100 F or more.

Buster put the brothers up at his villa, an ex official residence of one of French Somaliland's distant past governing administrators of this tiny French Colony.

Air Djibouti's somewhat flamboyant Clark Harrington, or "Captain Buster" as practically everyone referred to him since departing Nairobi that day, had it made in the shade. His villa's full time staff, consisting of a gardener, a cook, and three pretty (by any man's standards) 'maids' all bowed and scraped to the character as if he was not merely lord and master, but **God Almighty** himself. Then to really compound this show of supercilious nonsense Buster, at the regal like wave of his arm (to his loyal subjects) said: "**Ma benediction a vous tous**." (my blessing to all of you)

Buster couldn't resist showing off his bedroom to Jammie and Banjo, an outrageously gaudy replica of his conception of a bedouin chieftain's harem.

At sight of this scene the brothers, unable to hold back a moment longer, broke into fits of laughter.

"Buster, I've got to hand it to you, you've got an awful lot of class for an Okie." Banjo burst out with, laughing like mad.

"Ya gotta admit it's kinda homey....an sheeit, they's nothin else ta do in this godfasaken ass hole of creation....don't cha know!?" Buster said with a little chuckle and wink of his eye.

Three days later, back aboard Air Djibouti's one and only old Gooney Bird, our two Herjolfsson's now well rested and, considering everything, reasonably content, once again, were heading north toward civilization. Bumming another ride with Buster, this time to Cairo, with an invitation to stay at his residence for the night, the brothers realized

they were approximately half way back to where they'd started from on this trip.

Buster's residence in Cairo was a small apartment, though very nicely furnished by the exquisite taste of his Egyptian wife, Tahiya, a beautiful woman, and quite obviously of very high Egyptian culture.

After a nights rest and while enjoying a late morning hearty breakfast with 'Captain Buster and Mrs. Harrington, Buster asked the brothers if they'd mind ferrying a C-47 to Beirut, Lebanon. Air Djibouti had recently purchased a left over relic from World War Two that had been sitting idle in Cairo for ten years. The plane was an unconverted straight military cargo C-47 that Air Djibouti was going to convert into a passenger version DC-3 civil airliner. The work was to be carried out at Middle East Airline's maintenance and engineering base at Beirut International Airport, an aircraft facility with excellent credentials in the performance of major repairs and aircraft conversion programs and even complete airframe overhauls.

There wouldn't be any pay for doing the ferry but it would add a bit more toward their on-going, if some what exotic, quest to reach northern latitudes and the hope for better possibilities of finding work.

With nothing to lose they readily accepted Buster's unique way to help them stay the course, while also relieving Buster the time and effort of having to perform the ferry himself. It was a very timely and convenient way of thanking their host, benefactor and

newly acquired friend while helping themselves along their way.

"I darn well preciate ya doin this for Djibouti an me... now when ya get inta Beirut I want ya ta get on down ta the **Kit Kat Club**....right there on the waterfront....fact is it kinda hangs part way out over the ole Med...ya know what ah mean!...Well anyways I want ya ta look up a friend a mine, names Russell Raft, so naturally we all call him **'Riff Raft'**....a real goer of a guy...ha ha ha ha...Oh sorry! Was jus thinkin back ta last time me an ole Riff partied at his partment....somabitch we did it up proud with a couple a his **Kit Kat** girlie friends...belly dancers ya know...An oh, I most forgot, Riff's partment is right on top the Kit Kat, so's ya can't have trouble findin the place...ha ha ho ho....yall's gona love ole Riff, an he'll take care ya from there...guaranteed!"

Nine

RIFF'S APARTMENT was enormous, well furnished in mostly Danish modern, lots of nice paintings adorned the walls and each one was the work of a local artist or by artists throughout the Mediterranean, Mid East, and Africa. There were numerous bedrooms each with individual bathrooms. The place was actually a large home not merely an apartment, as Buster inferred, and Riff owned it.

"I wanted a place near the water, night life, and big enough to not feel cramped...know what I mean?" Riff said as he invited the brothers in and showed them around. "I want any pilot down on his luck, or what ever, to feel he's got a roof over his dome as long as he wants to stay with me....sort of a lame birds roost....and I've sure been there, my friends...without a roof, I mean....you know what it's like in the flying game cause I can see it spread all over your faces....But you're home fellas, and for as long as you want so pick a room and throw your stuff in there and then let's have a little aperitif before I take you down stairs to meet some of my family...OK!?"

To describe Riff as the carefree, happy-go-lucky sort would be to fall considerably short of the mark. For a picture that would offer a bit more clarity to this characters true personality, allow me: Riff had been flying C-46's for Air Jordan out of Amman when he got fired for having a **"less than positive attitude about his work"**. Apparently Riff's carefree style fell prey to the less than pristine character of various station agents within Air Jordan's route system, and most particularly so on the Beirut - Amman segment.

Because of Riff's easy going ways, his cheerful outlook about life and love for all the mortal souls around him made him an easy target to take advantage of. To make matters worse Riff placed minimal emphasis into abiding by "operational rules established by people who do not fly airplanes for a living, pencil pushers and the like,"

Here's what happened: These slippery agents, after filling the plane to maximum capacity in passengers and freight, for paperwork purposes, would then add on extra people and/or freight **unmanifested** and pocket the revenue. Naturally these station agents dearly loved Riff and would always be overwhelmed with joy when he was assigned to flights they were assigned to handle.

The day of reckoning swept down on good old Riff one fine day when a Jordanian Civil Aviation Inspector happened to be aboard Riff's plane in Beirut on a return flight to Amman after he had been on a personal visit to Beirut.

The inspector, seated in one of the 52 passenger seats, with every seat being occupied,

was amazed when twenty additional passengers boarded, each carrying small foldable canvas camp stools, opened them and sat themselves down in the aisle way. The inspector, nearly speechless, finally got his voice up and running well enough to ask the elderly lady sitting next to him on one of the stools: "Pardon, madam, have you ever done this before....I mean, sit in the aisle?"

"Oh yes, many many times...always with the good Captain 'Riff'...he charges half fare for the aisle, you know!"

"Hey, Riff, how come you got so nonchalant with your loads at Air Jordan?" Jammie asked one day , after they'd been staying with Riff long enough to have gotten pretty well acquainted with each other.

"Heck, Jammie, I didn't start out that way....it sorta got a little outa hand after awhile....I'm a sucker for a sad story.... the agents used to ask if they could put one extra poor devil aboard....usually an old duffer who had to get somewhere or another on account of his sick grand mother, sister, lame donkey, or some such sad story, and usually the bugger supposedly had no money....You know, probably all a bunch of crap, but that's how these people are....Eventually I just gave up fighting it, you know....and they always treated me like I was the great Mohamed himself...to make matters worse."

"What the hell you going to do now?" Banjo said.

"Shucks, I've got one heck of a good thing going here... I buy beef and all kinds of European and American food products wholesale, and local fruit and vegetables, and then I sell the stuff to just about every American pilot flying in and out of Beirut....an they most probably add something on and sell the stuff to other folks, like down in Jedda, Riyadh, and Dhahran, Saudi Arabia, and Teheran,Iran and all over the whole derned Middle East. Heck, I'm personal grocery boy to just about every American and Limey pilot working in this part of hells little half acre."

"Well I'll be damned....a real life entrepreneur, and here my bro and I were feeling real sorry for you losing your job, Riff, you cagey bugger." Jammie said with a touch of awe to his tone.

It was no time at all before Banjo landed a job playing his banjo downstairs at the Kit Kat Club, and Jammie fell back to his old standby; playing poker.

After a few weeks of enjoying the carefree life of a bum in Beirut the brothers were told about Iranian Airways needing pilots in Teheran. Riff had gotten this information after delivering a huge load of groceries to an American pilot flying for Iranian Airways, and passed it on to the boys.

Ten

AFTER CONTACTING the Beirut station manager of Iranian Airways Jammie and Banjo quickly received free passage to Teheran for interviews. From the station manager they learned the airline was in quite a pickle over their need for pilots.

Each interview lasted less than eight seconds while pilot licenses and medical certificates were checked, after which the chief pilot shook the brothers hands and said: "Welcome aboard Iranian Airways, gentlemen."

Once they had finished filling out the usual umpteen different employment forms they were taken to a hotel on Takhtjamshid Street. The small (about sixty five feet square by five stories high) affair constructed with building blocks made from a mortar of mud and straw, then sun dried, was the standard in building materials of the time. In many public buildings within this general part of the world, where building codes did not exist, there were no steel reinforcing rods utilized in the structures.

Checked in and their bags unpacked they found a quaint little restaurant nearby that specialized in French cuisine, an especially nice discovery the brothers agreed was a good indication their luck was starting to improve. When it comes right down to it there is only one thing in the world secondary to a beautiful and sexy woman, to the average male being's thought process, and that is definitely **'good food'.**

After a great dinner with a fine bottle of French wine the two hit the sack feeling greatly relieved over, once again, having found gainful employment. Looking forward to a good night's rest, and just before dozing off Jammie said to Banjo: "It sure feels good to be getting back on track, doesn't it!?...I guess they'll start giving us some transition training tomorrow in the DC-4...probably a couple hours to work the rust out of our down time...don't you think!?"

"After half that bottle of Burgundy I'm not going to try thinking about anything except getting a good night's rest for a change, brother dear...goodnight!"

It was around three-fifteen that morning that the airline crew busdriver entered their room and loudly announced: "Wake up please Captain Jammie and Captain Banjo, please! We must depart this instant for flight control...and your luggage must be with you!"

"What kind of a stunt is this, if I may be so bold to ask?" Banjo, now sitting up in bed and showing signs of deep consternation.

"Captain, you must hurry to come with me....your flight departs at zero four-

hundred hours....quick, I help pack bags....you dress, sir, then we go quickly, please!"

Their ride to the airport was strictly white knuckle all the way, with a tire screeching stop (reminiscent of a base ball player sliding into home plate on his stomach) in front of Flight Operations (Flight Control / Iranian Airways terminology). It seemed like the driver was out the door before the van even came to a complete stop, racing to the luggage rack and grabbing the bags while yelling: "Quick, Captains, we must hurry into flight control!"

The brothers were wide awake and had been ever since the driver took off from in front of the hotel like they'd been shot out of a gun.

Jammie said to Banjo, as they were hurrying into Flight Ops: "Have you got your breath yet, bro?" Followed by: "Wow what a crazy bastard that driver is, eh!?"

"This whole thing is beginning to remind me of those old Laurel and Hardy films back in the thirties...remember?"

"Right, you've got it."

They departed Teheran on the daily DC-4 service to Abadan riding as passengers after having been told they were to be domiciled at the new base in Masjid-i-Sulaiman, an important oil field location 150 miles north of Abadan,

About an hour out of Teheran the brothers had just finished a breakfast of tea, goat cheese, a good sized piece of chappatis (unleavened flat bread), an orange and a banana, and some kind of fish that didn't look or smell good enough to take a chance on, when Banjo decided to recline his seat back and try to catch some of the sleep they'd been denied. His eyes were closed and he was nearly asleep, when a sudden shaking of his shoulder brought him back to consciousness. He looked up to see one of the pretty flight hostesses looking down at him with a very frightened look about her. "**Captain!, oh Captain!**..can you fly this airplane, please, oh please sir?... The pilots are very ill, food poison I think.....Both pilots are unconscious...Ohhhh pllease!"

Jammie, at the window seat and now fully awake after hearing this wild story looked at his brother as they both started out of their seats asked Banjo: "You ever flown a DC-4 bro?"

"Ask me that again when we get into Abadan."

Entering the cockpit the first thing they saw was the copilot doubled up in a fetal position on the companionway floor obviously unconscious. The Captain was sitting in his seat, legs drawn up to his chest, moaning and groaning deliriously, tears running down his face. When the captain saw the brothers he instantly grunted out the words:"Get me out of the fuckin seat and head for Abadan, fast!...They gotta a good hospital there... You guys got any time in fours?"

"Yea, Capn, we're well qualified." Banjo said as the brothers proceeded to remove the Captain from his seat, which turned out to be a hell of an effort because the guy was a giant of a man and the way he was all doubled up, and in such pain, made it even worse trying to move him.

"The fuckin fish I think." The captain blurted out as they lay him on the floor just ahead of the copilot. The hostesses took over then and tried to comfort the two as best they could, but it looked like the copilot was dead.

Banjo slipped into the pilot seat and looked the situation over discovering that the plane was on auto pilot maintaining level and stable flight with the altimeter indicating an altitude of 13,000 feet.

A little over an hour later, shortly before starting their descent to make a "Radio Range" instrument approach into Abadan, in a rapidly deteriorating weather condition that had developed into one heck of a sand storm, Banjo asked Jammie to call Abadan Control to request a descent clearance, and to alert them of need for an ambulance to meet the plane upon arrival.

Jammie, glancing over at his little brother wrestling the big four engine airliner down the final approach to Abadan's runway, the plane gyrating wildly in that hellish turbulence and piss poor visibility brought an enormous surge of adoration over him for his brother. It was the first time he truly realized what one hell of a man this little brother of his really was and it made his heart swell with joy and wonder. Here he was, flying a big DC-4 for the first time in his life, and Jammie knew this for fact.

To compound things beyond reason, Banjo managed to grease those tires right onto that runway so perfectly it was amazing, after which he glanced over at Jammie with a sly smile and a kind of smart ass wink.

"Jeez, Banjo, that cuts it you show off little son-of-a-gun, you!" Jammie said laughing.

"This ol girl doesn't feel all that different from my dearly beloved ol Lancaster, easier in fact with the nose wheel steering, I might add."

The copilot did die, but the captain survived and made it back to the line after several weeks in recovery. It was rotten fish the cockpit crew had eaten. Fortunately for the passengers they hadn't been served the same food .

Eleven

It WAS like 'old home week' when Bat Marlow and Harry Hampton learned of their arrival back in Abadan, and because of the spectacular way they had arrived they were welcomed as heroes. A great banquet at the NIOC officers club was given in their honor that lasted until the wee hours, with booze flowing like a great **Tsunami**.

The brothers were put up for the night at Harry Hamptons house, which was actually around two o'clock in the morning by the time they got to bed, bone tired and well oiled.

At 4:15 , less than two hours in the sack, Harry, after considerable prodding and rather loud vocalizations managed to wake the two sleeping 'heroes' and advise them they were to be flown to their new domicile, departing in two hours.

"Holy mackerel they sure keep lousy hours around here." Jammie said as they floundered around in the bedroom looking for their clothes and trying to ignore the onset of magnificent hangovers in the making.

Banjo, with a weak little chortle, said: "Looks ever so much like we've been banished from civilization by the great one upstairs, brother, dear."

Arriving at the air terminal our heroes were more than a little surprised to learn the flying machine they were traveling to Masjid-i-Sulaiman in was not merely an old airplane, it was an antique from the earliest days of British commercial airline operations. "Where in the heck did you dig that old derelict up from?" Jammie asked Harry, as they proceeded toward the plane, carrying their bags.

"Don't knock the old sweetheart, she's going to serve our new oilfield operation darn good, and you're going to grow to love her same as you'd feel about your faithful old dog.... I guarantee it." Harry said with a convincing smile.

The deHaviland DH-89A Dragon Rapide, a wood and fabric biplane with 9 passenger seats and a single pilot seat, is a product of the early 1930's. It's all-up weight was 5,000 pounds. Powered by two deHaviland 225 horsepower six cylinder Gypsy Queen inverted inline engines, it had a top cruising speed of 160 miles an hour. As a short haul utility transport and navigation trainer it was widely used throughout World War Two in the European theater of operations primarily.

When the Herjolfsson's were hired, in Teheran, they had assumed they would be based in Teheran and would be flying DC-3's and maybe later, DC-4s. In reality, with a slight bit of pre planned forgetfulness no mention had been made that they were actually hired to open up and operate a new station at Masjid-i-Sulaiman, or 'M I S' as the place was ordinarily referred to.

Establishing M I S as a flight crew and aircraft emergency maintenance facility was deemed necessary by the airline. As it turned out no one in the company would agree to a transfer to such an undesirable location.

It boiled down to where they had to recruit new hires. People from outside of Iran and without a clue as to what they were actually getting into would be required. Basically it was a twentieth century version of the old "**Shanghai**" technique for manning and facilitating Iranian Airways', Masjid-i-Sulaiman's base.

Enroute, about half way in their one hour flight to MIS, with Harry piloting the Rapide, he pointed out the airfield for Ahwaz, the only city between Abadan and MIS, with a warning about the ends of the macadam runway having a sheer drop-off to the surrounding sand of a foot or more. "If you land slightly short of that runway surface, your going to end up sliding down that hot black tar on your buns, gentlemen. I guess what I'm sayin' is don't land short!" Harry said and laughed quite loudly.

MIS was a dismal outpost in foothills at an elevation of 2,100 feet, and had a population of about 18,000 people, most of which were of the Bakhtiari tribe. The first productive oil well in the country was brought in at this site in 1908 by the British. The city grew from that point to a large oil production field.

The road between MIS and Ahwaz and on to Abadan was usable only during the summer months as much of the desert between MIS and Abadan was flooded in winter by heavy rains making surface travel impossible except by camel or donkey. Consequently an airfield was built in 1929, and it was this airfield the brothers were destined to bring back from it's present state of many years of neglect to that of a fully serviceable and functioning airline terminal facility. A line of work neither brother had any training for, nor any idea what they were soon to be thrown into, like it or not.

What had happened to cause the airport facility to be in such a state of disarray was the Shah's nationalization of Iran's oil industry in 1951, and throwing out the British management and operating group. Rumor had it that the Shah believed his country should be receiving a larger piece of the action, that 20% of the take was the reverse of how it should be for Iran's share. As well it may have been, but the rest of the world took sides with the British, the folks who discovered the oil and built the operation up to be a major producer to the worlds growing hunger for petroleum products. The refinery at Abadan was one of the largest of it's kind in the world and a major supplier of high octane aviation fuel for the allies during WW II.

Unfortunately for the Shah the rest of the world's oil producing countries established a boycott against Iran. No one was to buy Iranian oil, or do business of any kind with Iran.

It wasn't until 1954 that a compromise was worked out with help from the United Nations whereby a consortium of oil companies was formed to run the operation. This consortium included an American oil company, British Petroleum, Royal Dutch Shell, and Iran's National Iranian Oil Company.

Under the consortium arrangement everything was headed toward Iran's recovery from those three years of isolation from the rest of the world, but it wasn't going to be an easy recovery because the entire infrastructure of the country was in shambles, and MIS airport was in one hell of a mess. Nearly every window in the passenger terminal, airplane maintenance hangar, and airfield maintenance shed had been removed by the locals and taken to their homes in town, some three miles distant.

Every room in the terminal building was empty except for tons of sand that had accumulated from seasonal sand storms.

The airplane hangar and adjoining maintenance shops were disaster areas of decay and destruction that made one wonder how anything was going to be salvageable.

Almost exactly one hour from takeoff at Abadan Harry dropped down to 3,500 feet and flew over Masjid-i-Sulaiman to let the town know they were going to have a visitor, and to give Jammie and Banjo a glimpse of their new home town.

"To say that MIS might resemble the back side of the moon would be too kind....in fact it looks more like Dresden when the Eighth Air Force got done with it." Banjo said in a dreary tone.

Now swinging over the airfield to look for a wind sock and not finding one, Harry buzzed the dirt and loose gravel runway surface about ten feet above the ground to get a look at the runway for debris and then pulled up while banking sharply to the left to look back and learn which way the wind was blowing the dust he had made.

The wind was negligible so he continued around in his left turn to a downwind and a few minutes later made a perfect three point landing touching down almost on the very approach end of the 2,500 foot long runway.

After parking in front of the forlorn looking passenger terminal Harry told the brothers, from his pilot seat, he wasn't going to shut down the engines, and that the mayor would be arriving shortly to pick them up and get them squared away in their living quarters in town.

As the Herjolfsson Heroes took this in they were wondering how marvelous life was treating them in their chosen field of aviation. Here they were at the very pinnacle of their professional lives, right here in beautiful Masjid-i-Sulaiman's marvelously manicured aerodrome, with their immediate boss anxiously waiting for his two idiots to get the hell off the airplane so's he could shag ass outta' Dodge right pronto.

Just before Jammie started to walk down the aisle to get off the plane Harry handed him an envelope and said: " There's a list of MIS people with job titles to be contacted in town along with a rough idea of how to go about establishing an operations base," and then with a big smile, "Welcome to Shangrila gentlemen!...Give me a call on your telephone once you're settled in and ready to give er' hell fellas!" Harry said as they were about to step down and out of that deHaviland DH 89 A Dragon Rapide rocket ship.

"Yea, right, Harry...will do." Banjo said, but was thinking; **'you meant Shanghai you fucker'** as he and his brother stepped out of the plane.

The brothers were barely clear of the tail as Harry gunned the engines and quickly swung the old Dragon Rapide out and away from the Herjolfsson Heroes. In his haste to be up, up, and away from the place, it was no secret that Director General Harry Hampton didn't appear too interested in staying at Masjid-i-Sulaiman any longer than absolutely necessary.

"Have you got that same feeling I have about our boss not being all that fond of this unbelievably lush little place in quaint and sunny Iran?" Banjo asked his brother, who was currently involved in a coughing fit and spitting up loads of sand after Harry's prop blast had nearly blown them away in a suffocating cloud of sand filled dust, and four years worth of other filthy debris that had completely buried the macadam parking apron.

In between great fits and spasms of coughing and choking, Jammie said, "I've got to admit, you've hit on an irrefutable observation, Sherlock."

As Harry and his trusty Dragon Rapide gradually faded away into the western horizon, the brothers, still standing there on the wind swept apron, were both silently fighting an inner turmoil of hopelessness, despair, and self denunciation.

" The downward spiral appears ever tightening, Jammie, but as you no doubt noticed not before we had found our true Shangrila,....right here in the middle of nowhere."

No sooner had he gotten those words out of his mouth when the sound of a car came roaring out of the distance at very high speed. The enormous billowing cloud following behind it was not merely huge, it was an ugly amalgamation of dust and particles of debris that had collected on the road from years of disuse.

What came sliding onto the dust covered tarmac, brakes squealing loudly and the tires screeching to a stop, was a great big black Rolls Royce limousine, vintage around 1938. A magnificent machine if ever there was one, even if it was carrying more dust than would seem fair and just for such a fine automobile.

The driver jumped out the instant the Rolls came to a stop, some ten feet from where the startled Herjolfsson's stood, and raced to open the passenger door for the single occupant.

"Welcome to Masjid-i-Sulaiman my dear gentlemen." The Mayor was small and frail looking in his too large and baggy black suit and 'Top Hat'. But congeniality by the ton was the guys outstanding quality our boys were soon to realize. It turned out the Mayor spoke no English beyond that initial welcome greeting, or at least nothing they were able to dissect from his babble that interpreted to English. Consequently, all the way into town the brothers just nodded their heads, as if they understood Mr. Mayor's mangled attempt to communicate with them.

In the Mayor's office they met Mrs. Mayor, a very handsome woman who was about twice the size of Mr. Mayor, spoke good English, and welcomed the brothers warmly. "Gentlemen, your arrival in Masjid-i-Sulaiman has been very long awaited, I assure you...and it is very good you are **American** flying officers....We hope your visit with Iranian people is very good."

The brothers politely thanked their new hosts, after which Mrs. Mayor spoke to her husband in Farsi, and with easily interpreted gestures that the brothers understood told him to transport them to their new home.

High on a hill overlooking the ragtag looking city of Masjid-i-Sulaiman the Rolls Royce limousine passed through a massive stone and mortar archway with a long and narrow gravel driveway that ended after about a quarter of a mile in a roundabout.

The car slowed to a stop by an ornate wrought iron gate that was open. Mr, Mayor hurriedly got out of the car and proceeded to remove the brothers bags from the rear luggage rack, after which he beckoned them with a huge smile to follow him. With amazed expressions on their faces over the magnificence of their new home, they stepped down from the Rolls and followed Mr. Mayor up the marble stairway and through an elaborately ornate stone and mortar arched entryway. The front door was a massive affair of fine hardwood, with equally massive wrought iron hinges, as was the door opening fixture.

The building itself was constructed of huge multi colored native stone and mortar. It was single story, and though it had a flat roof line, there was a corrugated iron pitched roof built over it that was fully opened under the eaves all around, obviously as an effort to shield the sun light from direct contact with the primary roof, and allow air to circulate freely.

The walls of the building were one meter thick., again, another attempt at staving off the dreadful summer heat common to the Persian Gulf, where 143 degree Fahrenheit temperatures, and higher, are not uncommon.

From the Mayor's pigeon English they learned that their new home was the Sheikh of Ahwaz's summer palace. The old Sheikh used Masjid-i-Sulaiman's 2,100 foot elevation to escape from some of the fiery temperatures of Ahwaz's summer heat. Though the140 temperatures existed in that whole general area, Ahwaz felt much hotter due to very high humidity created by it's close proximimity to the Karun River immediately to the West, and the Persian Gulf to the South. This high humidity of the atmosphere in the Abadan and Ahwaz areas was treacherous when combined with those ungodly high temperatures, and though M.I.S was only 2,100 feet higher in elevation it was nearly 100 miles further inland from the Gulf's wretched humidity.

The combination of very high temperatures and air so super saturated with moisture creates an affect upon human beings not unlike that of suffocation.

Though their new abode was quite large, nineteen oversized rooms in all, eight of which were bedrooms, tile floors in a light shade of green throughout, a mammoth sized and very comfortable sitting room (by any standards), and furnished to the hilt with old fashioned style English overstuffed settees, numerous lounge chairs with ottomans, and walls lined with book shelves (minus the books), and golden shades of expensive looking drapes were hanging from the high ceilings at all windows.

The dining room table of marvelous and ornately styled hardwood had seating for sixteen people, but with room to spare for several additional places. There was definitely nothing within the entire palace that would give one a sense of crowding or cramped for space.

The grand old place gave the brothers a feeling of stepping back at least one hundred years into English antiquity, but this Sheik's palace was not up to the grandeur of an olden times English bigwig's class of residence by any means. Even so, it was the swankiest residence that either of the brothers Herjolfsson could claim as their personal domicile.

The brothers gradually adapted to life in this wickedly harsh spot on planet earth, managed to refurbish Masjid-i- Sulaiman's airport facilities, and eventually had the place fully operational.

Along the way they had endeared themselves with practically everyone in the city and outlying villages within the entire Bakhtiari tribal region. Iran's Bakhtiari's are a proud and wonderfully talented people. Their carpets are true works of art, very tight and finely woven, and beautiful in their hues of red, yellow, green and blue.

In order to get the airport squared away as soon as possible the brothers hired practically every able-bodied man, woman, and child in MIS. They even created jobs that weren't entirely necessary for the building of goodwill and a close relationship with the people of MIS. A daily sweeping of the runway might have been considered ridiculous by anyone from the outside looking in. But, it put a lot of people to work who hadn't had a steady source of income for most of those years Iran had suffered through the outside world's boycott. against their country.

M I S was quickly to become a major cog in Iran's oil production under Iran's newly formed "Consortium", a compromise plan worked out between the Shah and a group of the world's major oil companies. Under "Consortium" management the newly formed framework of the National Iranian Oil Company was up and running in record time and efficiency.

Iranian Airways's oil field commuter service division was to play a vital roll in the overall success of Iran's reentry as a major supplier to the world's ever increasing hunger for oil.

Within a few months of the Herjolfsson brothers arrival in MIS, and the surprisingly fast transformation of a derelict airport back into a functional facility, a fleet of five DH89-A Rapide's were operating daily passenger and freight service between a network of seven oil field production sites. Two Rapide's would depart from MIS each Saturday through Thursday. Friday being the Moslem Sabbath, no flights were scheduled, but aircraft were available for emergencies and special charters.

The routing of the flights were as follows: One plane departed MIS for Agha Jari, Gach Saran, Bandar-e Mah Shahr, Abadan, Ahwaz, and back to MIS. The second plane flew the same stations in reverse order. Once a week, on Saturday's, round trip service to Basra from Abadan was added to the flight schedule.

Two more American pilots and a British mechanic arrived at MIS during the second month of operations completing the complement of personnel for MIS's flight operation, and fully occupying the living quarters of the old Palace. Jammie, being slightly senior in age to the others, assumed the unofficial head of household and company operations manager's job, and additionally fell into another responsibility; that of doing the cooking out of need. None of the others could cook or, most probably out of sheer laziness, claimed they couldn't.

This was asking way too much of the self assumed MIS station manager. Within a few weeks time, and with help from the good Mrs. Mayor, a cook was brought on board.

Karim, a small and frail looking fellow around thirty years of age was very happy to be employed in service to a hosehold of expatriates once again. He not only was all smiles at the first meeting, the interview, he talked a mile a minute about his cooking expertise, how he learned English family cooking from his past employer. Karim had served a British family for many years, in fact right up to the demise of British favor in Iran's oil industry.

Karim's mangling of the King's English was decipherable, but just barely. Jammie and the others, when asked their opinion about the would be cook, were all game to give the guy a shot at the job. When Karim was told he was hired his eyes glazed instantly, he then grabbed Jammie's right hand with both of his giving it a mighty shake followed by a deep bow, and "**choukran, choukran, choukran,...jazeelan ya bey**!" (thank you, thank you, thank you,...to you sir!).

Harry Hampton, when Jammie consulted with him about MIS's dire need for relief from the domestic requirements of MIS domicile, laughed and said: "Jammie, you're the head honcho up there, do what you have to do to try and maintain a happy household on that side of the moon." Harry then placed his hand on Jammie's shoulder and with a big grin said, "Thanks for taking that awful load up there off my back...you and Banjo are good folks...Just send me a note on what you need to cover expenses up there and I'll pry it out of old money bags up in Teheran."

Things settled down to a reasonable degree of normalcy from that point on at the MIS operation. With this said an explanation about the choice of words,"**reasonable degree of normalcy**", needs a bit of clarification. Living in this very isolated part of the country, (the **world** more aptly said) took a lot of adjusting for expatriates from the West, the more up to date part of the world.

One day after Banjo had flown a circuit of the route system, fresh from a nice bath, and now relaxing in one of the old fashioned overstuffed lounge chairs in the living room, he was catching up on news of the outside world from his two week old copy (actually quite current by MIS standards) of the British "**Guardian**" newspaper left aboard the plane by a recent arrival in Iran from civilization. Newspapers were like gold to our boys in exile on the back side of the moon.

Lounging there as comfortable as heck, enjoying his paper, he suddenly noticed out of the corner of his left eye a mouse running by and under the chair across the room facing him. These old chairs had skirts of ruffled material around them that nearly reached the floor. Banjo had been sitting with his left leg crossed upon his right knee, the paper spread out before him. Quickly, and quietly as possible, he put the paper on the side table, slipped his lounge slipper from his left foot with his right hand and slowly and as silently as he could manage, raised the slipper above his head as he approached the chair. Now, down on his knees in front of the chair he reached out with his left hand, very quietly secured ahold of the center of the chair's wooden frame and with a quick lifting motion tipped the chair over backward. The object being to surprise the mouse under the chair and clobber the bugger with quick action of the slipper coming down on the little devil's head. Bravo, with this superior line of thought? Not only no, but Hell no!

To the chilling surprise of our great white hunter Banjo saw no mouse waiting patiently to be beaten to death. With his right hand raised high above his head, slipper in hand ready to strike a deadly blow, our hero saw a streak slither toward him at lightening like speed, strike a vicious blow to the crotch area of his trousers, then struggle to wiggle free it's fangs from the tight woven material of his trousers.

Finally extricated from the crotch of Banjo's pants the snake scooted between his legs, over his left ankle and disappeared behind him somewhere.

His heart pounding furiously, hand still raised high above his head with the slipper still in a tight grasp, Banjo was frozen in shock. The sight of all that had just occurred, the feel of the reptile slithering over his bare ankle, and the thought of where the vile thing had gone within the house, were the shock of a life time.

He soon recovered enough to call out for Karim to come help locate the snake's whereabouts. All other members of the household had yet to arrive from work but would start to show up at any moment.

"**Karim, we have a snake in the house...we must find it quickly**!" Banjo excitedly exclaimed loudly. Karim didn't understand what he was so all worked up about until Banjo demonstrated by making a zig zag motion with his hands near the floor from where he had been sitting.

"**Snak snak snak snak!!!!**" Karim suddenly screamed aloud and ran from the room when he finally understood what Banjo was so Godawful worked up about.

"**Where in hell are you going, Karim**?" Banjo called out as Karim departed the scene, with Banjo close at his cooks fast moving heels.

Karim had gone straight to the servants bungalow near the back of the palace grounds.. Unbeknownst to Banjo, and anyone else for that matter, Karim's quarters, as of that very same day, was now being occupied by his wife, Nabila, their four year old daughter, Leila, and his brother-in-law, Ahmed. Entering his house Karim called out for Ahmed to come quickly to help find and kill the snake.

Banjo, slightly taken aback when he looked into the house over Karim's shoulder and saw the three strangers staring back at him with frightful alarm written on their faces. Alarm, primarily, because they had been told by Karim not to be seen until he had asked and received permission for their being at the palace, and secondly on account of Karim's excited tone in mention of the word "snak".

Ahmed immediately came running from inside the house and grabbed a walking stick that had been leaning against the wall near the entranceway while Karim also produced a similar stick from just inside the entryway of the bungalow. The three men now took off at a dead run to start their perilous mission to eradicate the snake from the palace. It wasn't until later in the day that it became quite clear to all expatriate members of the household why it was that practically everyone in Masjid-i-Suliaman carried a walking stick. The whole area was a living snake haven. Our dauntless airmen were soon to learn that several varieties of Cobra's, Viper's, Krait's, Scorpion's, Camel spiders, and other deadly creatures abound here in our **Valhalla.**

This particular afternoon of snake hunting, **<u>inside</u>** the intrepid aviators 'home-sweet-home', turned into a long, frightful, and most grueling experience for all concerned. It was decided that Karim and Ahmed perform the actual room by room search, they being experienced from a lifetime living amongst the deadly creatures. It was well after an hour of cautious and thorough searching, room by room, every crack and cranny, under mattresses, the bed springs, in closets, and armoires, every seemingly potential hiding place before an excited Ahmed screamed out at the top of his lungs from Jammie's bed room: **"Karii...mm, snak snak snak, hone!"**(Karii...mm, snake snake snake, here!) Herjolfsson's, and by now the rest of the flight staff had all gathered, and were standing around in the living room awaiting word from the servants that they had found and killed the snake. It is reasonable to surmise that these men were quite ill at ease (an understatement to be sure) with the newly realized knowledge they were sharing their home with a deadly reptile.

Shortly Karim and Ahmed entered the living room with the dead snake grotesquely dangling at the end of Ahmed's stick. In unison the living room gang yelled out in relieved tones to their voices: **"Hurrah, Hurrah, Hurrah!"** Now in the center of the living room, everyone cautiously gathering around to get a guarded look at the little bugger who had so dramatically disrupted the day at Iranian Airways MIS crew domicile, Ahmed, his facial expression indicating very serious concern stated flatly: "**Krait!**"

Ahmed had found the snake living in the bottom of the console that held the old British made Philco refrigeration type air-conditioner. Each bed room had one of these units located opposite the foot of the bed. Spacing between the foot of the bed and the unit, which was against the wall, allowed for about a three foot passageway.

The thought of walking past that air-conditioner numerous times, on bare feet and legs, a snake whose bite is so deadly one has a mere three or four minutes to live if bitten,

was reasonable cause for Jammie to come a bit unraveled.

"Karim, I have a few things that need to happen as fast as you and Ahmed can do them, number one: Find out how the damned snake got into the house! Number two: Plug up the hole, crevice, or what ever it was! Number three: Get rid of the mice and rats the snake was feeding on! "

Sleep that night was basically a washout for the whole gang. This led to a bunch of weary guys trying to do their jobs following the day of the big snake in the house scare. Banjo was thoroughly traumatized over the ordeal of actually experiencing a deadly snake strike out at him and bite into the crotch of his pants, then slither away between his legs and across his bare ankle. The poor devil had deteriorated down to a near basket case, listlessly dragging himself through his work days, not getting enough restful sleep, being deluged with frightful nightmares.

This condition went on until the house had been fumigated with burning sulphur, a suggestion by the Mayor, to rid the house of all vermin. With no more rodents running freely about the house, Banjo eventually returned to his good natured and happy-go-lucky persona. However, it is doubtful he ever fully recovered from that dreadful scare. Every once in awhile he'd wake up in the middle of the night in a cold sweat swearing that he'd felt a snake slither across his left ankle. But those occasions gradually became farther and farther apart.

It was several days before the snakes source of entry into the house was discovered, even though everyone concerned was searching with extreme diligence to the cause. Then one day, Bishop, the British aircraft mechanic had a brain storm: He wondered if there might be room enough for a small snake to get in through the hole in the wall where the main plumbing line passed through. That was it. The hole through that meter thick wall was nearly two inches in diameter, the pipe one inch outside diameter. More than enough space for snakes to slither through the wall. Oddly enough the water main pipe entered the Palace through Jammie's bathroom just ahead of the front end of the bathtub, an area concealed from view by wooden mouldings.

This was quickly alleviated by applying mortar to both ends of the hole in the wall, and with that now accomplished everyone slept somewhat better.

Next up, in one of the on-going series of thrills the men were experiencing in their exciting life at "Shangrila" Iranian style was when Jammie finally got up enough courage to ask Karim why the chickens he had been serving for dinner had such a distinctly **different** flavor from cooked chickens everywhere else in the world. Fact of the matter was that all the crew had quietly expressed disparaging remarks about Karim's version of baked chicken.

Early on in life with Karim, the men learned quickly of Karim's fragile nature. His feelings could get hurt over the slightest indication he was being distrusted, or not performing his duty perfectly. He'd start crying instantly if he felt someone was displeased by him in any way. Consequently everyone tended to go overboard with praise for his work.

It turned out that Karim, and apparently all the people in Karim's world cooked chicken with the guts and all **still in the carcass, and left them in there at serving.**

Jammie nearly fell over backward on learning this choice bit of news. Recovering from his shock and gathering his wits about him he tried hard to think of a way to tell Karim in a way not to hurt his feelings; that Americans remove the guts before cooking chickens.

Little Karim looked up at Jammie as his eyes started to water, followed by a heavy grimace as he struggled desperately to hold back from showing the depth of the sorrowful hurt he was feeling. He just stood there, his mouth shut tightly. It was as if he had gone into shock.

Jammie felt terrible. Not knowing what to say or do that might soften the blow he quietly turned and left the kitchen, allowing Karim to find his own way out of his pain.

Months later after numerous adventures with violent sand storms, mechanical problems with the planes, and the continuous ordeal finding palatable food, things suddenly took an unexpected turn that was to change the lives of the Herjolffson's drastically. Before getting into that, it's worth mentioning something about the on-going ordeal concerning food for the crews at MIS Station. Food buying was pretty much a daily thing done by Karim in the early morning hours shortly before sun up at the Bazar Square in the town's center.

Karim had to buy his daily supply of freshly butchered Goat, Camel, or the occasional Water Buffalo meat before the blowflies woke, at first light. This was important because the flies would descend upon the uncovered meat in swarms, lay their eggs and soon maggots infested the meat. Refrigerators at MIS were nonexistent at the time. There was no such thing as storing highly perishable food. One simply shopped each day for that day's supper meals. The breakfast menu never varied from a piece of unleavened flat bread, chicken eggs, and tea, unless one of the flight crew staff stumbled across some oranges or other fruit that Harry managed to secure via hook or crook once in awhile.

After dinner dessert at MIS was either a bowl of locally grown dates, a pomegranate, or pistachio nuts. Occasionally Karim would serve some kind of a concoction made with dates, goats milk, and some kind of a spice, or spices, that looked good in the little bowls it was served in, but that was where the reference to "good" ended. It tasted terrible, and smelled as if something in the ingredients had spoiled.

Finally, by consensus, it was time to tell Karim to forget about serving the stuff. Naturally, no one wanted to be the one telling, overly sensitive, Karim this. It was again Jammie who got himself coerced into the dirty work by being "senior member of the household and acting general manager of MIS station", as they put it. The cowards had ganged up on him. And yes, poor little Karim cried like a baby when this was laid on him, even though Jammie again tried desperately to tell him the dreadful news in a way that would not be taken too harshly.

In the instance regarding the "**very disgusting**" tasting dessert Jammie learned, Karim had been using a baking lard he'd purchased in the Bazar, a local by-product he learned from Karim was made from goat and sheep fat. That was bad enough, but what capped the climax was learning the producers of this ugly looking dark brown colored sludge, with it's nasty odor, were storing it in, and marketing it from leftover World War Two 55 gallon steel fuel drums.

Twelve

LIFE HAD been pretty rough for the people of MIS when the British departed. The local economy had been based almost entirely on the oil related business at MIS. Through those three years between the British being kicked out and establishment of the Oil Company Consortium, people like Karim suffered severely. In fact, it was later learned, Karim and his entire family nearly starved. Seems he was the principal bread winner for not merely his immediate home, but that of a whole string of relatives who looked upon him as their savior.

As hard as the whole household tried to convince Karim he was not going to lose his job over his failure with that horrible tasting dessert, nothing seemed to work in trying to console him. The guy was devastated and eventually it reached the point where Jammie had the Mayor and Mrs. Mayor come to the palace and explain to Karim in Farsi that his job was not only secure, but that they would not be able to get by without his excellent services, and that he and his family were loved by all the men.

.Finally something worked and normalcy returned to home-sweet-home and to the great relief of all concerned. It was then that a unanimous agreement was made to try not to rock the boat again with any of the servant staff. It simply wasn't worth the giant disruption to everyday life it seemed to cause.

The people of the remote areas in Iran, like those of Masjid-i-Sulaiman for instance, were basically ignorant of the world outside their immediate little place on earth. At least this was so in 1954-55, the era of this story. One day when Banjo was talking with Karim over some irrelevant thing or other, Banjo had made a flippant remark about the world being round. Karim instantly countered with: "Flat, Captain Banjo... no round say you!" With a big smile and demonstrating with both his hands out stretched in front of him he made sideways motions with his hands and kept repeating the words: "**flat no round**". These simple people still thought the world was flat, and to prove it, Banjo was led by the hand to the road out front of the palace where Karim pointed toward the horizon across the flat desert with the sun gently setting below Karim's "**flat desert**" world.

No matter how hard Banjo and the others tried to explain about the world being round, etc., they finally gave up in frustration. Jammie suggested they try finding a globe of the world sometime when in Teheran to try getting the idea into Karim's head.

Life settled into a routine of monotonous round robins in the Dragon Rapide's and equally monotonous days and nights at the palace until while diverting widely from course to avoid a nasty thunder storm, on a flight from Gach Saran to MIS, Banjo spotted a shiny C-46 parked at the end of a long ago abandoned airstrip below him. No one else aboard saw it, as the plane had flown directly over it. Banjo saw it for only a few seconds before it passed from view under the nose of the plane. He quickly noted the time and kept very close track of his further headings and times in order to back track to the site later. The airstrip was not represented on any current flight charts and probably had been abandoned prior to WW II.

Without mentioning his discovery to anyone on return to MIS he was on pins and needles while waiting for Jammie to arrive from his late afternoon Abadan shuttle. Meanwhile, Banjo had plotted a spot on a current chart as close as possible from the data he had recorded while making numerous changes in headings to avoid thunderstorms that day. First, he plotted the various course lines and their corresponding mileages in reverse order from MIS back to the approximate spot on the chart where he placed an X. Then he drew a circle around it with a twenty five mile diameter. The C-46 had to be somewhere within that 25 mile circle.

Jammie was secretly having a hard time believing there would actually be a C-46 sitting out there in the middle of nowhere when they went out to look for it. Why hadn't they known about this before he wondered? He did concede to the possibility that the reason was because of the strange site location Banjo had so meticulously plotted. The location was considerably outside the normal flight path for this segment of the airline's operation, and it was that which made it plausible in Jammie's mind.

They decided to wait until Friday, the Moslem Sabbath, a holiday for everyone at MIS, including the airline's staff. Friday came two days later with the Herjolfsson brothers taking off in the Dragon Rapide at dawn after telling the airport custodian they were going Pheasant hunting. Harry Hampton had readily given his permission for use of the plane for bird and Wild Boar hunting as an incentive to help toward keeping his MIS staff reasonably happy being stuck in such a remote outpost with nothing in the form of leisure time entertainment.

Flying Banjo's plotted course they spotted the plane's shinny aluminum sparkling in the early morning sun. Within ten minutes they were passing directly over the mystery plane, and right on the ETA.

"Well, I'll be damned Banjo, thar she are!" Jammie's voice was heavy with emotion as he spoke these words, standing behind and looking over his brother's shoulder at the controls of the plane.

After buzzing the landing strip a few times just a few feet above the surface in order to get a close look at it's potential for landing with the relatively small wheels of the Rapide , they both agreed it looked OK.

Banjo touched the Rapide's wheels down at an airspeed as slowly and gently as humanly possible, the old bird creaking and groaning loudly as if she was very unhappy about being put through this totally unfair ordeal. It was definitely a rough runway surface for the small wheels of a Rapide, but for the giant balloon like tires of a C-46 it could be considered reasonably serviceable.

Before entering the plane they walked around it while looking for obvious reasons it would be sitting there in the first place. Especially so after noticing that the plane had probably been refueled from the twenty four empty 55 gallon drums now laying off to the side of the airstrip.

" It sure looks like they've got her ready to go....all those empty drums over there, doesn't it Jammie!?"

"Let's look inside. Maybe there's an answer in there."

After rolling one of the empty drums over to stand on to reach the doorhandle Jammie managed to pull himself up and into the plane with Banjo's help.

"Holy mother of God"! Jammie burst out aloud, nearly falling over backward from the doorway.

"What's wrong, Jammie"? Banjo said with a startled tone to his voice.

"The smell in here is enough to kill a horse, that's what's wrong."

Jammie lowered the stepladder lying just inside the plane to Banjo who quickly crawled up and said, "**Wow!**...now isn't that just a dandy aroma!"

The horrid stench was coming from two dead bodies inside the plane, both of whom appeared of Asian heritage in their early twenties they judged. The brothers believed the two young men to have been the pilots, possibly the sole occupants of the doomed flight. It appeared they had died from the effects of exposure to the extremely harsh summer heat in this vast expanse of sand and dunes for miles in all directions from the site.

"I think they simply sat here drinking their water supply up and died of thirst, Banjo. Just look at how their mouths have swollen and lips all cracked to hell..Jeez, what a way to go." Jammie spoke in a very subdued tone, the depth of his sadness apparent.

Their emergency water supply appeared to have been only a few one quart canteens, all of which were empty, as were the emergency tins of food rations.

"These two guys weren't exactly all that brilliant, were they, Jammie!?.....Heck, they could have walked to Gach Saran in only a couple, maybe three days with the food and water they had.....sure seems strange they sat on their asses and expired right here.... Doesn't it seem weird to you too?....I mean, they must have known they could have saved themselves by walking the thirty or so miles to Gach Saran."

"Either they were lost, didn't realize how close they were to civilization, or maybe it was a case of not wanting to be rescued for fear of being found... I'm beginning to think they may have been renegades running from someone or something over in South East Asia.." Jammie said.

"Yea, and the tail markings look like they were painted on in a hurry with a broom or some sort of coarse brush, and if I'm correct they're either Chinese, Burmese, or maybe

Laotian....something in that neighborhood, anyway." Banjo said.

After some sleuthing throughout the plane for clues to the mystery of where the plane and crew had originated, they discovered electronic equipment data plates had C.A.T. markings stamped on them, and inside a framed registration certificate holder they found the ownership of the plane to be a Mr."Wong Fun Moon", with an address in Hanoi, North Vietnam It was also noted that the logo on the letterhead of the certificate did not match that of the less than professionally painted tail markings.

The more they discovered in the plane and on the personal papers and property of the dead crew, the more apparent the story became that they had stumbled upon a C-46 involved in some sort of clandestine mission. A plane that had not been reported missing, had not been flying on a flight plan, must have been involved in something of an illicit nature seemed apparent.

The pilots had been dead long enough to have created an ungodly stench in the plane, and helped to convince the brothers they needed to get the two ripe corpses under ground ASAP.

After laying them to rest in the shallow graves they had scooped out of the sand with a piece of aluminum, the brothers stood beside the graves, heads bowed in prayer while Jammie spoke a eulogy: "Here, dear lord of us all, lie the remains of two mortal souls...two fellow airmen who have made their final landing in this place on God's great earth...please have mercy on their souls... Amen."

After covering each grave with a large mound of sand they fashioned grave markers with cairns of small stones they had gathered from an area off to one side of the runway.

The burial now completed, they returned to the plane to try learning why the crew hadn't flown out of the area once they'd refueled the plane from the 55 gallon drums they'd discarded along with the battery powered portable fuel transfer pump. The pump they'd probably used to transfer fuel from drums to the plane's tanks it was assumed. Deciding a more thorough search of the plane for clues was needed to try solving the mystery they each started opening service doors and hatches, Jammie in the front area of the cabin, Banjo in back.

Within a quarter of an hour Jammie called out, "I've hit pay dirt Banjo...come here!" What had happened was that Jammie became a bit discouraged after not having any success once he'd opened all the panels and looked in every possible nook and cranny he could think of, so he decided to sit in the pilot seat and try analyzing the crazy situation with what they knew for certain. But, as soon as he sat in the seat he knew it didn't feel right, so he got out of the seat and lifted the flimsy cushion aside to discover, to his great joy, a nicely made leather case of some sort, possibly an attache case he thought. Lifting it out from under the cushion he was surprised at how heavy it was. Opening it he was even more surprised to find several fairly large gold ingots staring up at him.

"Oh....my....God!" Banjo exclaimed in a tone establishing his absolute amazement at the startling sight of glowing gold he was staring at on the pilot seat.

Further examination of the carrying case disclosed a cleverly concealed secret compartment in the lid. This proved to be another breathtaking discovery once Jammie accidentally stumbled onto the unlocking sequence of steel pins that secured the cover in it's closed position. When the cover finally flopped open several passports fell out along with a lovely bunch of American **greenbacks** in bundles of $100 notes, and a sealed envelope.

Handing Banjo one of the bundles he said, "Count the notes, Banjo, while I look into this pile of passports."

While Banjo was counting the bank notes Jammie discovered that each passport carried the photograph of only one of the dead pilots, which struck him as quite strange. Why this one pilot had so many fake passports and the other pilot didn't made no sense, he thought.

Opening the sealed envelope, which held a handwritten address in French to someone in Prague, Czechoslovakia, Jammie pulled out a typewritten letter, also in French. With his High School knowledge of French he was able to translate the letter well enough to establish it as some sort of an informal requisition list for a variety of small arms weapons and ammunition. The letter also introduced the two pilots as direct representatives of the letters author, some Royal Prince from the Kingdom Of Laos.

"Brother dear, I now wish to announce that we are the proud recipients of an even one hundred thousand bucks in cool hard cash!"

"Kinda looks like we've stumbled onto some sort of hanky panky being played by a Laotian Prince....probably some unhappy idiot trying to take over his daddy's throne or something....at least that's my guess." Jammie said with a chuckle.

"What are we going to do about all this?....I mean, maybe it's time we shagged ass outa here while the gettin's good." Banjo said in a tone indicating an uneasiness Jammie also was beginning to feel.

"I can't agree with you more, Banjo, but first there's something real fishy about this bunch of passports here.... I mean only one of the pilots pictures is in each of em....the other bugger isn't shown at all...and that leads me to believe we've got another stash of

passports for the other guy....maybe more than passports, if you know what I mean?!"

They both then simultaneously grabbed for the copilot seat cushion, tugged at it until the snap fasteners were released, and there it was, another handmade kind of leather carrying case. It was nearly identical to the one found under the pilots seat cushion, even to the sealed envelope and it's letter.

"How heavy would you estimate the gold to weigh, Banjo?"

"Feels like around 60 or 70 pounds to me, what do you make it?" Banjo said.

"I'm with you...maybe even a bit more...and that would be times about fifty bucks an ounce in Luxembourg, I think." Jammie said with a look of astonishment on his face followed by, "Now, I'm all for us gathering up our winnings, getting back to dearly beloved MIS, and calling it a day."

Once on the ground at MIS they taxied the plane to the hangar and parked in such a way no one looking could see them unloading the loot and carrying it into the hangar where they stashed the leather cases in one of the unused steel lockers originally intended for safe storage of highly valuable aircraft maintenance tools. Next was to padlock the cabinet's door.

The sound of a car suddenly arriving at the hangar gave the brothers a bit of a jolt until it was found to be the crew car. The driver, on hearing the plane fly past town had dutifully driven out to pick them up.

"Banjo, why don't I go to the Palace and get the padlock from my footlocker and come right back while you hang around here to guard our loot !?"

Fortunately it was the Moslem Sabbath, none of the usual work force were present in or about the hangar. Only the air terminal security guard was on duty, and he hadn't moved from his post in the terminal building because he knew who had landed and had no reason to come out to snoop into what his bosses were up to.

While Jammie had the driver take him to pick up the lock, Banjo decided to weigh the two cases of gold. All told they had one hundred thirty two pounds of gold . Banjo now tried to mentally calculate their current financial worth. He reasoned that if Jammie was right about that $50 an ounce figure he'd mentioned, they were suddenly a couple of quite solvent gentlemen. After putting a pencil to paper he came up with the gold's weight in ounces at two thousand one hundred and twelve. Mumbling to himself as he quickly multiplied ounces times fifty, a great jolt of adrenalin hit his heart as the sum developed into a nice cool one hundred and five thousand six hundred bucks. Another shot of adrenalin struck again, this one nearly buckling him at the knees as he penciled in the two hundred thousand in greenbacks to the gold figure and stared down at the piece of paper with the numbers, **305,600** scrawled across it.

When Jammie returned with the padlock Banjo couldn't help bursting out excitedly with: "We've got one hundred and thirty two pounds of that yellow stuff, and if that fifty bucks an ounce is possible, we're talking one hundred five thousand six hundred Yankee dollars...and adding in the green stuff brings our current net worth to three hundred five thousand six hundred bucks worth of reasons to shove off for somewhere with a much more pleasant climate....wouldn't you agree?"

"Banjo, I can't help but agree with you, but first we've got to come up with a plan on how to get outa here with that one hundred and thirty two pounds of gold....and next there is the little problem of, **'where'** are we going to land and start over?"

Without any hesitation, it seemed, Banjo came out with: "Ireland....lovely green and cool old Ireland would be my choice."

"Then that's settled. It's Ireland where we'll settle and do our damndest to carve out a good life, brother dear!" Jammie said as they shook hands in agreement.

It was later that same evening as the brothers were relaxing in the living room after supper when Jammie suddenly asked Banjo if he'd checked the battery power on the Forty Six: "The batteries were dead....**hey!**, that might be the answer, Jammie. I'll bet they ran the batteries down so low with that fuel transfer pump they didn't have enough juice left to start an engine....That's what you were thinking too, wasn't it!?" Banjo said in an emotional tone of voice.

"Right, the poor devils drained their ship's batteries down too far before realizing their mistake...a deadly mistake for them....a godsend for us."

"I wonder if we oughta go back with a battery power cart and see if we could get the engines running...maybe bring it here and put our old India bird's registration numbers on it?.... what do you think?" Banjo asked his brother.

"I think if we were to do that, we best change the registration numbers where she sits, along with stripping that Indo China logo off her as well...Yea, Banjo, I think that's what we'll do....next Friday we'll go on another little "bird hunting" trip and see if we can catch us a dandy old Curtiss C-46 to bring home." Jammie said with a wink of his eye.

"What kind of a story are we going to cook up for the rest of the gang here, and at Abadan, to hopefully get them to swallow, may I ask?"

"Easy, we had a friend of ours in Beirut ferry it to Basra, where we took delivery and he flew back commercial to Beirut." Jammie said with another wink and also a big smile.

"It might work...for awhile anyway. Meantime we oughta let Harry know we're going to fly the coop soon so's he can find some other poor and innocent buggers to fly his Dragon Rapides." Banjo said.

"You're right, Banjo, but we aren't going to be able to sit around here very long before the old aviation 'grapevine telegraph' starts causing the hair on the back of our necks to stand up real prickly like....meaning we've got to have everything pretty well sorted out by next Friday, and soon's Harry gets a couple replacements on their way here, we're long gone."

Friday finally came, but it seemed like the longest week ever for the Herjolfsson's. All the way enroute to the C-46 the brothers wondered and worried about whether the plane would still be there, or that they wouldn't be able to get the engines started, and all sorts of other negatives kept plaguing them.

As luck would have it they had no problems starting the engines after hooking up the battery cart they'd brought, and after a run-up check found the engines, and all systems airworthy. Being convinced the bird was flyable they shut down the engines, and got busy spray painting over all the existing identification marks, lettering and numbers. For air pressure to operate the paint sprayer they'd brought a fully charged nitrogen bottle for that purpose. As quickly as the fast drying aircraft type silver nitrate dope paint dried sufficiently to work on they used masking tape and newspaper to form the identification

numerals and lettering of their C-46 from India. Once they had satisfied themselves the masking work for the lettering looked OK they sprayed on a non gloss black nitrate dope.

Within four hours after their arrival at the C-46, they were done with the paint work, had removed the masking tape and paper, and were ready to head for MIS.

All the equipment was now stowed aboard the Rapide, all except for the battery cart they would use to start the C-46's engines, after which it would also be loaded aboard the Rapide.

Just before Banjo was to board the C-46, he and Jammie shook hands, both brothers with solemn looks upon their faces. Wishing each other safe journey they climbed aboard their planes and flew uneventfully to Masjed-i-Sulaiman. The C-46 being considerably faster than the old Rapide, even under very low power settings being used, Banjo was forced to zig zag and even circle back and around the Rapide numerous times before arriving at a prearranged place approximately ten miles west of MIS. At this point Banjo would circle until Jammie landed and had time to open the hangar doors. This was to facilitate getting the C-46 into the hangar and out of sight as quickly as possible.

===== A Lineage Rekindled =====

The MIS staff living with the brothers at the Palace were told the tale of picking up the C-46 in Basra, Iraq, apparently not questioning the story. But to help prevent rumors from spreading wildly the brothers asked all of the airline's personnel to deny any knowledge of the C- 46 in the hangar other than it was the personal property of the Herjolfsson brothers.

Several weeks passed while the brothers performed their regular duties, but every spare moment of their off duty time was spent going through every system on the C-46, inspecting it for any deficiencies and when found, making the necessary repairs. All of this was carried out under the supervision and generous physical and moral support of the MIS station maintenance supervisor, one James Scott from Glasgow. James appeared to have taken a special interest in the C-46 project, possibly due to the obvious clandestine nature of the affair, but also because the Herjolfsson brothers C-46 represented a job potential in civilization somewhere. As time went by the entire expatriate staff of airmen at MIS station gradually became hands-on assistants in the project. With virtually nothing in the way of free time entertainment at MIS, other than playing cards or reading weeks old European newspapers, turning the classical old C-46 into a bright and shiny jewel became their element of entertainment.

Something that helped to generate interest amongst the whole crew was a remark Banjo let slip one night as they were taking a tea break in the hangar. He mentioned, in an off hand sort of way that he and Jammie were hoping to start an airline company in Europe somewhere, and this bird they were all helping to put into pristine shape was their one and only asset toward pulling it off.

This little remark created an enormous spark of enthusiasm amongst the whole crew, each one of whom saw a possibility for escape from the hot and desolate Iranian dessert via a job with the Herjolfsson brothers (hoped for) airline company in civilization somewhere. The fact of the matter was that anywhere away from the dismal existence they were living, and the boring flying job in fabric and wood relics of the 1920's, was a powerful reason to make a positive impact upon the Herjolfsson's. And they were most certainly accomplishing this as Jammie once remarked off handedly: "Are these guys trying to send a message across to us, or am I dreaming?"

"I think they want outa here as bad as we do..... Bustin their buns the way they are, and have been ever since they joined our party, especially lately, leaves little to the imagination that they want to go with us, it would appear."

"You know, Banjo, when you think about it, we've got a good start, the nucleus actually, for our airline in Ireland....a great mechanic, and enough tried and proven pilots to build something worthwhile....What do you say we ask em if they'd be interested in working with us to try building an airline?"

"From what I've seen in the way they're working their asses off on the old bird, and all, I see no harm in askin...yea, let's ask em!"

Later that night, after they'd quit working on the plane, and were getting ready to head back to the Palace, Jammie asked them to come into the hangar office and take a seat: "Fellows, Banjo and I sure do appreciate what you're doing for us on the old bird out there in the hangar....in fact, we're wondering if any of you would be interested in a little proposition we'd like to offer you....To make it short and to the point, my brother and I are going to try an create an airline company using that old C-46 out there....and we're wondering if you'd be interested in throwing in with us to pull it off?"

Near pandemonium broke out instantly. There was absolutely no doubt about their interest as indicated by the loud cheers and happy faces.

Jammie quickly asked for their attention, and the bedlam gradually subsided to the point he could speak: "Men, it's not going to be easy to create something we'll all be proud of.... and it's not going to happen instantly. There will be times when money is going to be short, I'm certain....I guess what I'm trying to say is....well, will you stick it out through thick and thin?"

There wasn't any doubt in the minds of anyone present at the meeting that Jammie and Banjo weren't going to end up with a successful airline. They were a team with the talents and determination to build an airline, and the atmosphere in that hangar office was thick with the sweet fragrance of success in the offing. This fine amalgamation of airmen, their hearts and souls just soaring, couldn't possibly fail they all believed.

The way each man understood what had just happened was that it was a true rarity, a nearly unbelievable gift being offered. A foot in the door of a brand new airline. To be one of the first names on any airline's seniority list, even before the company actually got officially started was a once in a lifetime opportunity for any pilot in search of a career flying position.

Thirteen

THE REMAINDER of the Herjolfsson's time in MIS was a hectic period of sweat and fear that their plans would be quashed somehow or other. Finally, the day after having checked out their two new replacement pilots, the day they had previously told Harry would be their departure from "Shangri-la", as Harry had referred to the place at the beginning, they rolled the big bird out of the hangar just prior to sunset, and topped off the fuel tanks in readiness for an early departure the following morning.

Over dinner with the nuclei personnel of their future airline company, a company yet without a name, the brothers promised to write with details of their progress in getting certified to operate and established enough to start bringing them on board. There was a mixture of joy and sadness at the table. Every man wanted to jump ship, then and there, and leave with Jammie and Banjo on this great and exciting adventure.

"Men, hang in there!...Be patient and as soon as we can manage, you're going to get a call from us to give Harry your resignation notice and shag ass outa here to help us build one heck of an airline!... And you've got our word on this." Jammie spoke in a tone that left no doubt in the minds of all concerned that this would truly come to be.

The Herjolfsson brothers had mixed emotions about leaving MIS and Iranian Airways, partly because they had been given a job when they were in desperate straits for work at the time, but this had been greatly depreciated by misrepresenting the actual job they were to be assigned to. From flying the high and mighty DC-4's to being shoved off to nowhere's vil and the old rag and wooden Dragon Rapide's was a bitter pill to swallow.

What goes around comes around, it is often said, and it had come around for Jammie and Banjo Herjolfsson the following morning as the sun was just about to cast it's fierce but life giving rays over the rugged Zagros Mountains to the East.

While Jammie performed the preflight "walk-around" inspection on the bird Banjo telephoned in to airways communications center his flight plan for a direct flight to Beirut with a request to receive their clearance to enter Iraqi airspace by radio after takeoff. The request was granted and the Herjolfsson's were now clear to "shag ass outa Dodge", as the saying goes.

Finally airborne, engines purring like fine swiss watches, all systems working perfectly, they settled back in their seats and enjoyed an enormous sigh of relief as Banjo gently banked the plane toward Basra on their westerly course, and glanced back at Masjed-i-Sulaiman barely visible through the morning haze.

"I hope we know what we're doing, Jammie....I sure do." Banjo said, looking over at his brother, after they'd completed their 'Climb Checklist' procedures while passing through thirty five hundred feet in their climb toward their cruising altitude of eight thousand feet and a course direct to Basra, direct Damascus, direct Beirut.

Now cruising at eight thousand and about fifteen minutes short of passing over Damascus Banjo picked up the microphone and called Beirut Center requesting a change in destination and a clearance from overhead Beirut to Nicosia, Cyprus. This caused a lot of confusion with Beirut Center being a less than always cooperative communications service, and especially so in dealing with pilots who spoke with an American accent. They were half way between Damascus and Beirut before finally receiving their clearance to proceed to Nicosia and with who to contact for descent clearance, etc.

The reason they planned the flight this way was to bypass potential problems with Lebanese civil aviation authorities in event suspicion should arise over a C-46 flight out of MIS, a totally unheard of situation in Middle East's air traffic system previously, as Abadan was the principle point of departure for international flights from southern Iran. Banjo and Jammie gambled that Cyprus would be the most likely international airport for a non-scheduled and non-commercial aircraft to receive permission to land as long as they were on a flight plan from Beirut. This way Cyprus would not necessarily take particular heed to their original departure point from MIS they hoped. Fortunately that is how it went for the Herjolfsson's at Nicosia.

Quickly, while Banjo handled the fuel and oil servicing requirements and gave the bird a good 'walk-around' for anything haywire, Jammie went into the flight operations and weather office to file a flight plan for Geneva.

Arriving in Geneva fourteen and a half hours since departure from MIS they decided to spend the night rather than trying to make it all the way to Dublin as planned originally. They were quite bushed, as much for the long day of flight as for their frazzled nerves over something of a negative political nature occurring. And there was also the potential constant for a mechanical problem with the bird throwing a monkey wrench in the works. As much as they wanted to get down on Irish soil it just was not logical, they needed a good rest before pushing their luck further. It was off to a first class (very expensive) hotel on the shores of Lake Geneva as soon as they'd serviced the plane with fuel and oil for an early start the following morning.

"I don't know about you Banjo, but I could eat the ass end out of a whole cow right now....what do you say we kinda splurge on a great meal with some premium wine, the whole works...huh Bro?"

"Sure sounds like the best plan of action to me...yep, and it just so happens we can afford a little treat...thanks to those unlucky guys laying back there near Gach Saran."

A great dinner, several toasts to the two dead Asian pilots buried in shallow graves under Iranian sand, and a full twelve hours of sound sleep later, the early morning start long gone, they managed to get airborne at a quarter past two pm.

After a little over an hour en route one of the Automatic Direction Finder navigation radios started acting haywire so Jammie went back to the electronics bay and removed it from it's securement rack. He thought the plug-in contact points might have been corroded and cause for it's erratic behavior. What he found when he removed the ADF were a number of plastic bags containing a white powdery substance. They'd been jammed in snugly between the various electronic parts of the unit. He realized almost immediately, to his utter disdain, that he was looking at enough deadly heroin to ruin the lives of an untold number of human beings. The dead guys had been smuggling dope from Laos' "Magic Triangle", one of the world's most infamous heroin producing areas.

Excitedly he hurried to the flight deck to break the news to Banjo. "What the hell do we do with this shit, Bro?......there must be a gigantic fortune jammed into that damned ADF.

They agreed without any hesitation. Within a few minutes Jammie had dumped the powered source for human sorrow into the flare chute where it dispersed into the atmosphere somewhere over France.

"As big a fortune as I just tossed into the wind, I've never felt so good and clean!" Jamie said aloud, and in a most solemn tone to his voice, as he returned to his seat.

"You know, Jammie, this little event sorta washes away those feelings of pity I held for those poison peddling buggers we buried back there in the desert!.....know what I mean?"

"Couldn't agree more, bro." It was only a few uneventful hours later when they landed in Dear Olde Dublin, Ireland.

"How's it feel to be home Jammie?" Banjo said as they taxied into the parking place the "FOLLOW ME" jeep had led them.

"I'll let you know once we've gotten through customs, immigration, and a few thousand other leaps and bounds we're going to have to handle with extreme care and intelligence if this is actually going to be **HOME**, as we hope it to be." Jammie answered with a solemn mix of fear and hope to his tone along with a somber expression on his face.

After clearing Customs and Immigration they took a cab into downtown Dublin where they found residence in a classical looking old Hostel called, "O'Shaughnessy's Inn". This was on recommendation of the airport "Handling Service's" customer relations representative, as most suitable to American aviators.

The instant the Herjolfsson's walked into "O'Shaughnessy's Inn", they felt strangely at home. It was as if they'd been there before. The homey atmosphere and friendly greeting they received, the aura of contentment all within seemed to exude.

"Jammie, why is it this place seems so darned familiar?.... It's absolutely eerie that....." Banjo was saying as Jammie cut him off: "I think I've got it....Bro, it's Xavier's '**GOOD TIMES**

BAR' all over again....dear old Luxembourg and Monsieur Antoine Xavier is what this place reminds us of."

"You're right, that's it....the same kind of a joint, the rooms upstairs over the bar here on the street level"

Todd O'Shaughnessy and his two daughters, Hazel and Heather, ran the place. Todd had inherited the Inn, as had three other O'Shaughnessy generations before him.

The place was perfect as far as the brothers were concerned, and though Todd was a gruff appearing fellow upon first meeting, the brothers were soon to learn he was really a big bluff with a heart of gold. Big in more ways than one, the guy was huge. Standing behind the bar like a gargantuan ape wearing a beer stained, and god only knows what else was on that raunchy looking apron, would scare off anyone of a timid nature if it weren't for the genuine smile perpetually plastered on his great big face. Todd was one of those oddly memorable kinds of people a guy never forgets throughout an entire lifetime.

Todd's daughters, in their early twenties, were nearly identical in personality to their dad, but one hell of a lot prettier. So pretty, in fact, the brothers nearly succumbed to apoplexy at first sight of the two buxomly endowed beauties while they were serving beer to customers throughout the barroom.

"Jammie, I feel like I just died and went straight to heaven....that gorgeous redhead is mine, and don't you forget it, brother dear!"

"Thank you. You know why?....cause she'll whip you into shape pronto....Christ almighty she looks mean." Jammie said laughing boldly.

"The brunette isn't exactly someone I'd kick out of bed, either." Banjo said while wiping beer foam off his nose after having paid too much attention to these positively breathtakingly beautiful young ladies and not enough to lifting his over flowing beer tankard to his lips.

"That, my dear friend, and baby brother, is my future bride!" Jammie spoke in a voice nearly inaudible. A voice Banjo recognized as his brothers when there could be no doubt about the seriousness of the matter.

With the C-46 in the shop being turned into a 52 seat passenger plane, every piece of equipment in it being overhauled to like new condition, the Herjolfsson's proceeded to fall in love over the next six weeks. They were both so taken by Todd's lovely girls, so hopelessly in love they'd practically forgotten everything else, including the reason for coming to Ireland.

"Heather, will you marry me?" Banjo asked as a tear suddenly ran down his cheek and onto Heather's as they stood in a tender embrace.

Heather then pushed herself away and with a straight and deadly serious face said, "If you promise to play the banjo for me always....yes, Romeo, I'll be your Juliet."

"Hazel dear, my brother and I are going to have a good life from here on out, and mine would sure be a heck of a lot better if you could see your way clear to share your life with me...would you?"

"Jammie dearest, if you wish to marry me all you have to do is ask " Hazel said smiling radiantly....of course there is father's permission and my dow``ry to consider."

"Will you marry me, Hazel O'Shaughnessy?......I've never loved anyone or anything so much...as I love you.!" Jammie, now down on one knee, spoke these words in his most serious and meaningful way.

"Oh, **yes yes yes** my Jammie, my dearest one, here, take my hand and let us go tell father.

Fourteen

OLD TODD O'Shaughnessy hadn't been blind or deaf to the obvious. On the contrary, he saw it coming long before anyone of the four of them had, he thought. In trying to think of a way to prevent the Herjolfsson brothers from taking his beloved daughters away to America Todd's agile brain was working overtime for a solution. Finally he had come up with what he thought to be a marvelous way to keep his girls from being whisked away to America, as well as doing something good for all the dear people of Ireland.

"I've got a proposition for you two hooligans, and I want you to hear me out first, then sleep on it before giving me your reply....right?"

"Sure, Todd.....wow, you sound really serious!" Banjo quickly answered.

"I am that....You two Viking heathens have a bad reputation here. Fact is it goes all the way back to the ninth century...if you know your history, that is."

"Geez, Todd, you aren't goin to shoot us if we run off with the girls are yuh?" Jammie asked, his smile giving way to a slight grimace

"Not exactly ." Todd said in a serious tone, but then gave himself away by breaking into loud and hearty laughter.

"Jammie, my boy, we need a holiday charter air service.... the Irish people would dearly love to get a week or two in the sun they advertise so much about of Spain.....To my mind it is right here in dear old Eire, I've been told, indeed I have, that your aeroplane can carry 52 passengers. They say you boys could carry people to Andalusia for half the fare of other aeroplanes, and much faster I've been led to believe....It would be a true opportunity to stay right here and operate a holiday charter airline, I do believe this."

"Hey, you're way ahead of us Todd, we've never thought about running an airline here in Ireland....Civil Aviation Authority wouldn't grant us an operating certificate, or would they?" Jammie said while crossing his fingers over his little white lie about their not having considered starting an airline in Ireland. Jammie had instantly realized it best to let Todd think it his idea they should settle in Ireland and operate a charter air service.

"Aye, lads, I've been told it is possible....many friends, regulars who drink in my pub, connections to the powers that be tell me it can be true." Todd said, the look on his face pleading desperately for the boys to not leave and take his little girls away.

"Todd, I am going to speak for the both of us, me being the elder of the Herjolfsson's here in Ireland....There is absolutely no need for my brother and myself to sleep on your idea. It sounds just great!....I assume you and your friends have been more than a little busy trying to dream up a way to hold us hostage here in this land of our dear mother's ancestry.... yep, Todd, my Mom's folks from several generations back are from dear old Ireland....Dad was a full blooded Viking, and a grander man never walked the face of the earth....Now, how many people do you have working on this **'grand and glorious'** little hostage plot, may I ask....sir?"

"Every bloody soul I know, and them's that they know.... some that's got weight in the ministries. Lads, I'm tellin yuh, stay in Eire, it'll be good to yuh.....I'll be givin all I can to your needs....you'll see!" Todd said, putting every ounce of persuasion he had in him to his plea.

Both brothers said thank you as one, and Jammie added: "It looks like a win win situation all around, then....how can we lose with all of Ireland on our side?" he said with a smile as he reached out to shake the hand of his future father-in-law, followed by Banjo doing the same.

"I believe this deserves a bit of a celebration." Todd said as he proceeded to fill three giant sized pewter tankards of Guiness's best beer. They celebrated uproariously till the wee hours and only for the sense of Heather and Hazel did the three of them get told to go to bed and sleep it off.

Fifteen

"**S**KYLARK OF IRELAND" was born and the airline became a huge success very quickly. A second C-46 was purchased from India and was in overhaul and conversion to passenger configuration when the brothers sent for Aunt Julia to be present at the double wedding ceremonies. The marriages were to be held immediately after completion of the required period of "courtship" under the rules for Irish based practicing Catholics; a minimum of one year according to the local Parish Priest.

Todd had developed a network of tour sales people throughout Ireland that was so effective Jammie and Banjo were amazed.

"How is it that you have dug up more people than we can haul...and after only a few months at it, Todd?" Jammie asked one evening over dinner at the Inn.

"Simple me lad. They get a pound note for each seat they sell, and if they sell fifty seats they get two seats free to use they selves, or they can sell em to somebody and keep the fares...

they cun make one hundred and eighty pounds a trip if they sell every seat yuh see...an that's why some oh my best lads are beggin me to get more planes." Todd said in an enthusiastic way that brought grins to the faces of all the family.

It was a week shy of the big wedding event, and the day Aunt Julia was scheduled to arrive in Shannon on TWA's Constellation flight from New York.

With Todd and the girls hurrying and scurrying in their preparations for a grand reception party at the Inn in Julia's honor upon her arrival, Jammie and Banjo felt compelled to get out from under foot of the O'Shaughnessys during the highly electrified atmosphere of the O'Shaughnessy domain. To avoid the flare up of Irish tempers the brothers, now free for a break due to having the first supplemental crew from the MIS pool of pilots trained to perform the trips to Spain, Jammie and Banjo decided to drive down to Shannon Airport early enough for a leisurely sight seeing trip through the beautiful countryside. Little time or opportunity had presented itself for this in the busy months prior. Now was a time to relax and fully take in the beauty and tranquility of a place on earth without equal. The majestic magnificence of Ireland was profoundly felt by the Herjolfsson's, not just the beauty of the land itself, but it's good and soulful people. Never had Jammie and Banjo felt so close and good and just plain comfortably at home as they now did in their adopted land.

Driving in County Kerry near Killarney the brothers came across countryside scenes of small farms with several different kinds of crops in a variety of colors reminiscent of a patchwork quilt. Then there was a serene area of lakes and mountains for a backdrop so beautiful it presented an aura of unreality about it. Stopping the car they both got out, and in the silence of awestruck reverie simply stood there taking in this glorious painting of nature.

The Herjolfsson brothers were experiencing something like two souls who had been traipsing across a vast desert for eons without water, then suddenly and miraculously an oasis of great splendor emerges before their eyes.

"You know, Jammie, I've never really experienced a picture in my mind of how heaven might be like, not until right now that is."

"Talk about Shangri-la....this has got to be ours.... Hilton must have been here to have found the inspiration it took to write his book, 'Lost Horizons'....it's exactly as I've always pictured it.... Look, even the little wispy clouds by the mountains there."

"Yea, Banjo, this is it...we're going to find a house or build one if we have to, right here somewhere with that marvelous view from the front window." Jammie said softly, never even taking his eyes away from the scene to look at his brother as he spoke.

A few miles further up the road they spotted an ancient building situated on a knoll some distance from the road. Stopping the car to get a better look at it they believed it to be an abandoned Fort or maybe even a dilapidated Castle. Quite large, but so sadly neglected and in need, quite obviously, of an enormously expensive restoration that it struck both men with a deep feeling of sorrow.

Leaning against the side of the car, both staring forlornly at the old relic, the once grand structure, thoughts started racing through their minds until finally, as if by some mysterious cue, they turned toward one another.

"Do you suppose?" Banjo asks in an unusually low tone of voice for Banjo.

"If we can buy it....I mean if it's for sale....how far are you willing to go to see it through?" Jammie asks of his brother.

"Dear Brother, all the way." Banjo replied.

"You're absolutely certain?" Jammie asked in a tone indicating Banjo's answer would be considered final with no turning back.

As close as the brothers had always been they had never felt compelled to shake on an agreement. It never seemed necessary nor appropriate. Neither had ever gone back on their word.

This highly emotion filled moment, a commitment to one another to turn a dream into reality, no matter what the cost or burdens might entail brought their hands together as they looked each other in the eyes.

They sped toward the nearest village in silence, engrossed in a kaleidoscope of deep thoughts, hopes, even prayers that they might find the owner of the ruin willing to allow them to turn a dream into reality.

The first village netted the name of the owner and where they could find him in Killarney.

Now running short on time to make it to Shannon and Julia's arrival they hurried to the address in Killarney only to find the man not in. The elderly lady who answered the door, the housekeeper, informed the brothers that "Mister" would be home from his work after his usual stop at the 'grog' shop known as "Macgillycuddys Revenge".

"It'd be foive, you'll foind the Mister at his grog." She said in a matter of fact yet pleasant enough way.

Time running out they were forced to leave, but left word with the housekeeper they would be back in a day or two to talk to the "Mister" about his property where the old building stood on the knoll.

Soon as the old lady said she would pass on the word to "Mister" they quickly took leave and high tailed it for Shannon Airport, arriving as Julia's flight was landing.

Aunt Julia cried great crocodile tears as she hugged her nephews. And, Jammie and Banjo were having a very difficult time holding back their own tears.

The O'Shaughnessy greeting turned into another very emotional event. It was almost as if these two families were one right from the moment Julia arrived on the scene.

Todd and the girls had done a fine job making Julia feel like a Grand Duchess with the reception and genuine warmth of this loving Irish family.

Something totally unexpected was how Todd was doting over Julia to a point the girls became a bit embarrassed at first. They had not seen their father act this way over any woman. Never, that is, except for that last year of their mother's bout with fatal cancer.

Eventually the girls, along with Jammie and Banjo found themselves happily amused at what appeared to be a mutual happening between Julia and Todd.

Never had the brothers heard their Aunt Julia giggle. Not in all their lives had they seen her acting like a young school girl....a girl who was obviously enjoying the company and special attention from a man.

This was a side of both, Julia and Todd, so very different from their usual personality traits it was extremely heartwarming to observe.

In the course of a mere two days two lonely souls had found one another, fallen in love, and though not admitting it were practically in ecstasy over the warmth and joy each was feeling for the other.

On the third day since Julia's arrival Jammie and Banjo excused themselves from the rest of the others and raced for Killarney to catch the "Mister" at his place of grog. They were hopeful that with enough grog in him it would lower any resistance he might hold toward selling the ruin. A ruin the Herjolfssons were dedicated to restore to their vision of how the magnificent old structure might have been in times of the long and glorious past for the family it had afforded grand shelter and well being.

"Mister" not only offered no resistance he shed tears to his overwhelming relief over the reality that finally he was going to be rid of the burden his family heritage had dumped on him. As owner and tax payer of a property referred to locally, in derogatory terms, as "Ravens Roost", but in better times had been called "Iris Hall" after a grand matriarch to our "Mister" William Macgillycuddy's clan.

The Herjolfsson's struck a good deal with "Mister", or "old Willi Mac" as he was known locally. Willi was regarded throughout the county as quite a colorful character, lovable, helpful, eccentric...etc. And, in regards to the Herjolfsson's a master key toward the materialization of a dream come true.

They promised Willi they'd return with full payment for the property in a week's time. The sale turned out to be for the entire estate, a considerably larger transaction than the brothers had bargained for in terms of acreage.

"Fifty thousand pounds is going to put us in the "Land Barons" category bro!...Do you realize we're upping the gentry status of our heritage by several notches, Jammie?"

"Aren't you getting a little carried away? We're still just a couple of renegade farm boys from Minnesota with airplane fever, and until very recently plagued with wander lust!... Remember, Banjo?"

"Jammie, yea, I remember, but for a few seconds there it was fun being a Baron or thinking about being called, "**His Lordship**", you know what I mean."

"Fifty thousand pounds is a lot of money, but for what it's going to buy for us, our whole darned family, it's peanuts for a ticket to heaven on earth, I think." Jammie said.

Nearly overwhelmed with joy and wonderment for their future, they raced back to Dublin, all along the way laying plans on how they would rebuild Iris Hall into "**Julia Manor**".

They decided to keep the project a secret until after the wedding, at which time they'd drive the whole family down to show it off. The drive, ostensibly to be a family outing to the South of Ireland for a few days of sightseeing for Julia. The first night, after their leisurely five and a half hour drive, they checked into Killarney Great Southern Hotel, a first rate hotel highly recognized as "The Grand Old Lady of Irish

Hotels". After check in, with everyone practically famished, they proceeded directly to the hotel's restaurant. It was during the course of enjoying a very delicious lunch when Jammie said, "After lunch let's take a drive around the area here, see the lakes, Killarney National Park and the Gardens...What do you say, folks?"

All were enthusiastic to Jammie's suggestion.

They cruised around the Killarney general area for nearly an hour enjoying immensely it's colorful and abundant flora everywhere one looked. At one point while driving near the shore of Lake Lean with Macgillycuddy's Reeks to the south west, Julia said, "I don't believe I've ever seen anything as beautiful as this lake with those magnificent mountains in the distance....water so blue and the mountains so lush and green....Oh, Ireland is like one grand garden...the entirety of it...it is simply breathtaking!"

Shortly after Julia had made those remarks the future **"Julia Manor"** came into view, the present remains of "Iris Hall".

It seemed like all three women spoke at once, one of whom shouted out excitedly: "Oh, my lord what a shame to see such a grand old mansion in such a state of dereliction...shame on it's owners, I say!"

"Jammie, please, can we stop and take a look at it?...Oh, please do!" Heather said in a pleading tone.

Naturally the car immediately came to a stop. The whole family then bounded up the knoll to get a close up view of what had certainly once been the home of a noble family. Now, with all six of the soon to be one family, standing on the front terrace of Iris Hall seemingly mesmerized by the breathtaking view of meadows and fields of maze below, the landscape off in the distance of azure blue lakes, mountains in numerous hues of green, and a sky so wonderfully blue with those billowy little white clouds floating gracefully by, Banjo couldn't wait any longer: "Folks, you're standing on the terrace ruins of "Iris

Manor", and I am happy to announce soon to become '**Julia Manor**'...yes, Jammie and I bought the estate awhile ago and have plans of returning it to it's original state of grandeur, back to when the place was at the height of Iris's time.

"Oh! my word...how on earth did you ....I mean, it is true? You boys are going to restore it to it's original state?....Julia Manor?... I don't understand !?" Julia said in a state of total bewilderment.

"Simple, Aunt Julia, as matriarch of this tribe it stands to reason the place should follow custom....therefore "Julia Manor" is to be the new home for all Herjolfsson's present and future.

Chapter 16

Six months later, a year to the day Jammie and Banjo arrived in Ireland, they celebrated the Grand Opening of Julia Manor. Lots of work still had to be done and a lot more money had to be pumped into the dream to bring it to fulfillment as the brothers envisioned their Shangri-La.

Once back at the old homeplace Julia wasn't having any success at all in her attempt to readjust to the solitude she had previously enjoyed, cherished actually, there at the old Herjolfsson family farm. Todd's image was a constant. His affectionate attention and the tender kindness he showered upon her was sorely missed. That particularly warm and comfortable way she felt while in Todd's presence was something altogether new to her.   Each passing day Julia's yearning for Todd's company had intensified to a point she began to think she was going mad. This lady, this dedicated schoolteacher who had given selflessly of herself toward the education of more than a thousand school children in her twenty five year teaching career had never experienced the wonderful, frightening, heart rendering nightmare involved with that crazy thing in life we commonly refer to as **"falling in love"**.

Once Julia realized what had happened to her there began a letter writing frenzy to and from Ireland ultimately leading to a proposal of marriage from Todd. Had this particular letter taken much longer than it had Julia was about to do the unthinkable. She had been in a state of utter turmoil over whether it would be considered outrageously improper for her to **"suggest"** a marital union with Todd in some way as to not sound too forward or brash. Would Todd think less of her if she took the lead?

Those wonderful little words, "Julia, my dear lady and soul mate, you belong here with us, with me. Please come and be my wife. I love you and want to be with you always. Please do, Julia my love."

After another three months of desperation getting the old home place sold, all accounts settled, in general getting all the loose ends taken care of in the process of closing out a lifetime in Minnesota Julia packed up and returned to Ireland where the love of her life awaited her.

In accordance with the norm for Irish "courtships" there would be the usual one year

before the marriage could take place - providing the Parish Priest was satisfied that both individuals were baptized, confirmed and were free to marry i.e., that they (one or both) were not being coerced and /or that they were not previously married. This included announcing in advance from the pulpit the proposed marriage to facilitate contact from anyone who would invalidate the proposed marriage.

Though Todd obviously was once married, the church's "previous marriage" rule did not apply here as his wife, the mother of Hazel and Heather, was dead, having passed away many years past from cancer.

Where one or both came from parishes outside of the parish selected for the marriage ceremony i.e., in this case Killarney, the Parish Priest of Killarney would have to ascertain exactly the same facts through contact with the respective Parish Priests in the couples home parish(es) - in their countries of origin.

All three couples were married on the first Sunday after satisfying Irish Catholic rules of courtship. In respects to Julia and Todd, it was a case where "exceptional circumstances" were applied by their Parish Priest allowing for the stateside months of physical separation of the couple to count toward the required year of courtship.

Though physically many thousands of miles apart while Julia was dutifully settling accounts she and Todd had maintained a constant flow of letters to and from. No doubt a decidedly different kind of courtship, but never-the-less an important part of two people

getting to know each other by their words flowing forth from the depths of heart and soul.

Immediately after the three couples emerged from the "Catholic Church of St. Mary of the Assumption", having completed their marriage vows they stepped into a Rolls Royce limousine and were taken to Kerry County Airport where they boarded a waiting **SKYLARK of IRELAND** plane which flew them off to jewel like and romantic little "**Ibiza**", an island located off the coast of Spain approximately one hundred miles south east of Valencia. Western most of Spain's Balearic Islands group, and not yet discovered by the hordes of tourists, Ibiza was the perfect place to honeymoon. Jammie and Banjo had carefully and secretly planned this as a special surprise for the rest of the newlyweds who had been led to believe they were going to honeymoon at a resort hotel somewhere on the Celtic coast of Ireland.

The cockpit crew were the first two of the MIS pilots called up to join SKYLARK, and who were now to reap the benefits of holding company seniority numbers just below those of the brothers, things like basking in Ibiza's sun, and all the other niceties one would associate at a premium class resort in the fashionable Balearic Islands.

The time of togetherness for this now formally united family in an atmosphere of fun in the warm and soothing sun of the Mediterranean, the great food, wine, and live music with every meal encouraged an overwhelming feeling amongst the entire family of sheer joy. They were experiencing a contentment with life itself, the truly good feeling that comes from a strong bonding between human beings.

The amalgamation of six individual souls forged into a family of three happily married couples now brought their thoughts into focus for the good life they each had ahead of them. It was a most sobering time of appreciation for the extremely good fortune each felt deeply to have found his or her soul mate for life.

Banjo said something one night at the dinning table gathering as the family were enjoying their usual aperitif in anticipation of another of the hotel's fine dinners. It occurred after he had had a particularly joyous day of fun in the totally relaxed atmosphere of that great resort when suddenly, and in a rather subdued tone of voice he came out with, "You know, folks...life has always been a deeply troubling mystery to me... really !...such a fleeting thing of ups and downs, good times intermixed with times downright awful....times when you meet some really good people and life is just dandy, then **BANG !**, some undesirable jerk or situation enters the tranquility and it's down in the dumps again...I can't help wondering if all this is just a great big pipe dream I'm having....something way too good to be true...something I'm soon going to wake up and learn it's all been another one of God's little taunting things designed for a purpose that completely escapes me."

"Banjo, me boy, I'm followin your line of thought completely...it's true, and for the life of me I can not understand why things happen the way they do, but I can tell you this, laddy, this is one hellova fine dream I'm not a goin ta wake up from, because it's Gods way of thankin each one of us for who we are in his eyes." Todd said this in such a dramatically touching way as to cause all eyes at that table to glisten from the tears that soon started to appear. For quite a few moments there was total silence in the electrified air hovering over that table.

The plain and simple remarks made by Banjo and Todd had stirred each of them to the very depths of their emotions.

It was at this moment when Julia suddenly realized the full effects of her implication in initiating the sit-down meeting with her nephews on that memorable day some three years past. Her actions to help the boys come to terms with reality made her proud of her heritage, but much more so for Jammie and Banjo themselves in managing to turn their lives around to such a degree of success she could hardly believe it had happened.

But happen it surely did, and with so many wonderful bonuses far and beyond that of the financial aspects hoped for at the inset. "Oh how very fortunate I am to live as witness to a lineage rekindled so heart renderingly", Julia was thinking as she sat there and counted her blessings.

Jammie realized it was now his time to make a statement. Pushing his chair back he stood up, and while collecting his thoughts he looked, in turn, from one family member to another then in a solemn tone of voice, "Folks, I want to make a toast to the one person at this table mainly responsible for all of the wonderful consequences that ultimately has led up to this moment - (now looking directly at Julia and lifting his glass to present her in a toast) - Aunt Julia, speaking for Banjo and me, we thank you from the bottom of our hearts for your wisdom, your compassion, your solution to help us out of the doldrums we had fallen into....raise your glasses please...**TO AUNT JULIA.**"

—The End—

Epilogue

THE ENSUING decade was a prosperous one filled with all the joys of life along with the occasional bouts with strife all people are challenged with in God's way of strengthening the bonds within a proud family.

Julia Manor's halls often reverberated from the wonderful sounds of children's voices at play - sounds that frame the meaning and warmth of home and give it life.

The airline thrived ten fold upon it's entry into the exciting era brought forth through the induction of jet airliners upon the worlds stage. Skylark's passengers were now being offered holiday excursions to an ever expanding variety of intriguing destinations over much of the world.

Through the speed, range, and economics of Douglas's magnificent four engine DC-8 and Boeing's 707, playgrounds formerly exclusive to the rich were now easily within the grasp of the middle income class of the Irish public.

Warm and relaxing places like Portugal's Madeira Island, and Spain's Tenerife and Las Palmas of the Canary Islands became favorites of Skylark's holiday trade.

Eventually the Herjolfsson brothers created a very streamlined type of airline operation. Greatly improved passenger seat economics was achieved through the use of high density seating and 100% load factors. These two basic parameters combined with operations restricted to the realm of charter flight only, hard work, common sense, and plain old Yankee ingenuity, Skylark set a trend for many other independent carriers throughout Europe to follow and prosper.

Capt. Tad Houlihan

About The Author

Born and raised in a small town in northern California's Sierra Nevada mountains, he started flying during WW II and at age 19 became a B-17 Flying Fortress pilot. After the war he found work flying for nonscheduled airlines until called back to active duty in the Air Force to fly C-54's on the Berlin Airlift. At the outbreak of the Korean War it was off to fly C-47's and C-54's in the Combat Cargo Command until his return to civilian life in 1953 and returning to civil air carriers, finishing his commercial piloting career as personal pilot to the president of a major US corporation based in San Francisco in 1990.

The author and his wife, Genevieve, have made their home in the US Pacific Northwest